Holt MUSIC

Eunice Boardman Meske
Professor of Music and Education
University of Wisconsin—Madison
Madison, Wisconsin

Mary P. Pautz
Assistant Professor of Music
  Education
University of Wisconsin—Milwaukee
Milwaukee, Wisconsin

Barbara Andress
Professor of Music Education
Arizona State University
Tempe, Arizona

Fred Willman
Professor of Music and Education
University of Missouri—St. Louis
St. Louis, Missouri

Holt, Rinehart and Winston, Publishers
New York, Toronto, Mexico City, London, Sydney, Tokyo

Special Consultants

Nancy Archer
Forest Park Elementary School
Fort Wayne, Indiana

Joan Z. Fyfe
Jericho Public Schools
Jericho, New York

Jeanne Hook
Albuquerque Public Schools
Albuquerque, New Mexico

Danette Littleton
University of Tennessee at Chattanooga
Chattanooga, Tennessee

Barbara Reeder Lundquist
University of Washington
Seattle, Washington

Ollie McFarland
Detroit Public Schools
Detroit, Michigan

Faith Norwood
Harnett County School District
North Carolina

Linda K. Price
Richardson Independent School District
Richardson, Texas

Dawn L. Reynolds
District of Columbia Public Schools
Washington, D.C.

Morris Stevens
A.N. McCallum High School
Austin, Texas

Jack Noble White
Texas Boys Choir
Fort Worth, Texas

ISBN 0-03-005327-7

7890 032 98765432

Acknowledgments for previously copyrighted material and credits
for photographs and art appear on page 221.

Table of Contents

To the Student

Many people think that only a person who wants to become a professional performer can enjoy the study of music. Actually, people of many interests and abilities can find great gratification in music. When considering how to learn about and be involved in music, you have many options. This book will help you to explore a number of these options.

Maybe you've thought about participating in a musical production. In Unit 1, you can learn about various ways you might be involved in a performance, such as composing and writing lyrics, singing and acting, preparing props and operating a video camera, or reviewing the performance. After you've learned how to put a musical production together, listen to the Broadway musical *Big River* and think about all the people who contributed to this performance.

Maybe you've listened to a piece of music and thought, What am I hearing? How am I supposed to listen to this music? Knowing how to listen can greatly increase your enjoyment of all kinds of music. In Unit 2, you can develop or refine your listening skills by learning about music from long ago and nearer to the present. On these pages, you can also focus on the parts of music –instrumental and vocal sounds, rhythm, melody, and texture. Then listen to three works from the world of musical theater—*The Play of Daniel*, *Madama Butterfly*, and *The Tender Land*. Has your musical ear changed? Are you hearing the music in a different manner?

Perhaps you've decided that you would like to focus on performing or creating music. Are you interested in vocal performance or in performing instrumental music? Or do you want to create new musical sounds? In Unit 3, learn about your singing voice: Find your vocal range and sing in different ensembles with your classmates. Continue in the unit, and learn to play guitar, percussion instruments, and dulcimer. Then apply your performance skills and make your own music, using classical, rap, and jazz ideas and such musical tools as the computer.

For many people, choral singing is their most important connection to the world of music. Unit 4 provides many opportunities to develop your choral skills toward a lifetime of singing enjoyment.

No matter where you focus your musical energies, you are certain to find some aspect of music that will be right for you. This book should help you to identify areas of musical involvement that you might investigate throughout your life.

Unit 1

Musicianship

The Many Roles

WANTED:	
COMPOSER	LYRICIST
CONDUCTOR	VOCALISTS
INSTRUMENTALISTS	CHOREOGRAPHER
ARRANGER	CRITICS
PRODUCER	PRODUCTION STAFF
TELEVISION CREW	

Have you ever stopped to think about how many people are involved in bringing a musical performance to life? Can you imagine how many different roles requiring musical skills must be filled?

Whether the final production is a single song or a full-length musical, many people have assisted in some way, taking on many different musical and nonmusical roles in order to ensure success.

Think about a recent performance you have attended, heard on a recording, or seen on television. Make a list of different musical jobs that had to be performed before the production could be heard. Then scan this unit and compare your list with the roles discussed here.

Consider the musical skills and knowledge required for each role. Which of these roles would you feel qualified to perform? In which would you like to become more involved?

My Lord

Words and Music by Joyce Eilers

Listen to a recording of "My Lord." What personnel were required to produce this recording? What tasks had to be accomplished? Learn your part of the arrangement shown on pages 7–9; then combine all the parts for a performance.

(melody) My Lord's gon-na come in the morn-in', My Lord's gon-na

stay through the night, My Lord's gon-na watch o-ver me, and

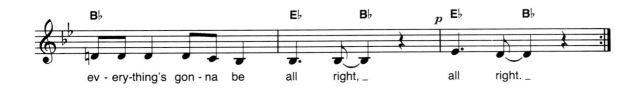

ev-ery-thing's gon-na be all right, __ all right. __

Divide into groups. Add the harmony parts to this refrain.

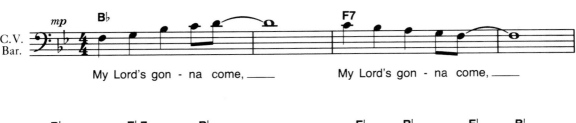

My Lord's gon-na come, _____ My Lord's gon-na come, _____

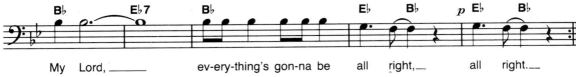

My Lord, _____ ev-ery-thing's gon-na be all right,__ all right.__

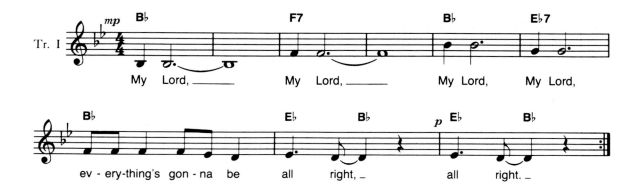

My Lord, _____ My Lord, _____ My Lord, My Lord,

ev - ery-thing's gon - na be all right, __ all right. __

Perform the song in this sequence: **unison** refrain; three-part refrain;
alternate verses with three-part refrain; coda.

1. Shad - rach, Me - shach, A - bed - ne - go __ in the
2. Mo - ses led the __ chil - dren of Is - ra - el
3. Lit - tle Da - vid __ flung a stone __ and

fier - y fur - nace were tossed. ____ Ev - ery - bod - y
down to the Red __ Sea shore, ____ Phar - oah and __ his
made Go - li - ath fall. _____ Man, you should __ have

thought their end _____ was near. _____ But __
ar - my close _____ be - hind. _____ Then the
seen his ar - my run. _____ Then the

they had faith __ that the Lord a - bove __ would
wa - ters part - ed, let Mo - ses through, __ but
chil - dren of Is - ra - el gave a shout __ and

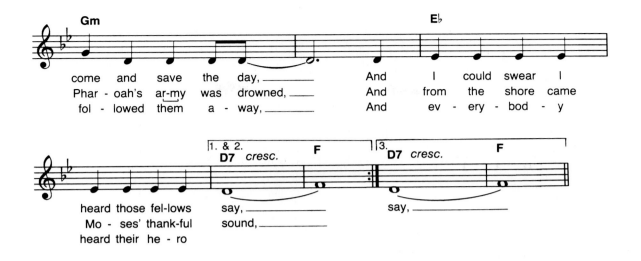

come and save the day, _____ And I could swear I
Phar - oah's ar - my was drowned, _____ And from the shore came
fol - lowed them a - way, _____ And ev - ery - bod - y

1. & 2. heard those fel-lows say, _____
Mo - ses' thank-ful sound, _____
heard their he - ro

3. say, _____

Coda

Tr. I
My Lord, My Lord,

Tr. II
My Lord's gon - na watch o - ver me, and

C.V.
Bar.
My Lord, _____

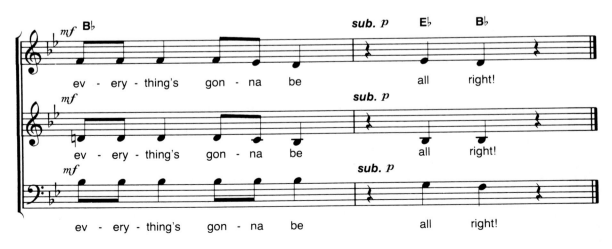

ev - ery - thing's gon - na be all right!

ev - ery - thing's gon - na be all right!

ev - ery - thing's gon - na be all right!

The Composer and the Lyricist

A musical performance begins with an idea. It might be some words jotted down by a lyricist . . . or a few notes of a melody that a composer devises.

The lyricist communicates ideas by choosing

- words that evoke images
- rhyming words for phrase endings
- words that create a natural rhythmic flow

The composer will express the text by

- following the natural rhythm of the words
- stressing important words by accenting them or by stretching them out over one or many notes
- choosing certain pitches to enhance the expressiveness or structure of the text
- selecting dynamics that create focal points and climaxes in the music
- composing a particular style of accompaniment to enhance the mood of the words

All of these elements are present in the song "You'll Never Walk Alone."

Can you discover how the composer and lyricist used these elements to make the music expressive?

You'll Never Walk Alone

Words by Oscar Hammerstein II

Music by Richard Rodgers

Tr. II

When you walk through the storm, keep your chin up high

C.V. Bar.

When you walk through the storm, keep your chin up high

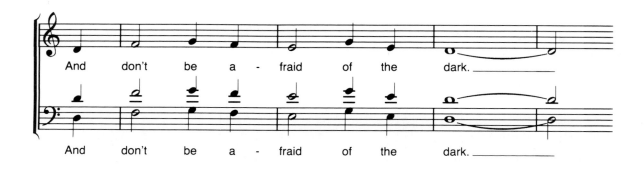

And don't be a - fraid of the dark. _____

And don't be a - fraid of the dark. _____

At the end of the storm is a gold - en sky

At the end of the storm is a gold - en sky

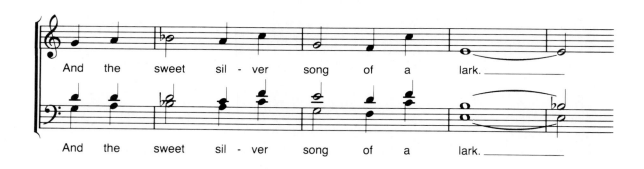

And the sweet sil - ver song of a lark. _____

And the sweet sil - ver song of a lark. _____

Tr. I
(Tr. II)

Walk on through the wind, walk on through the rain,

(C.V.)
(Bar.)

Walk on through the wind, walk on through the rain,

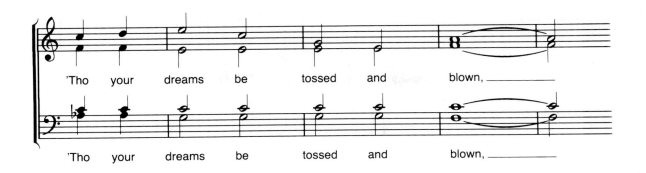

'Tho your dreams be tossed and blown, _____

'Tho your dreams be tossed and blown, _____

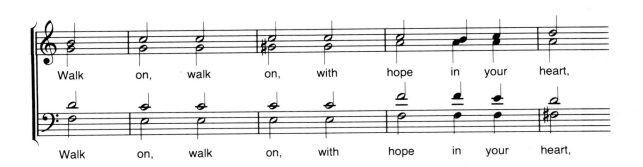

Walk on, walk on, with hope in your heart,

Walk on, walk on, with hope in your heart,

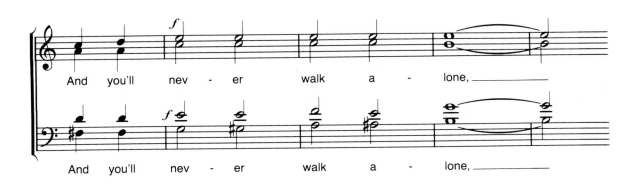

f

And you'll nev - er walk a - lone, _____

And you'll nev - er walk a - lone, _____

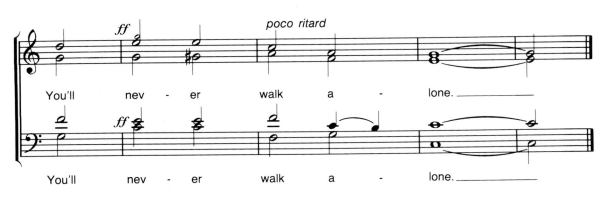

ff *poco ritard*

You'll nev - er walk a - lone. _____

You'll nev - er walk a - lone. _____

Good Night, Ladies

Traditional

Good night, la - dies, _ Good night, la - dies, _

Good night, la - dies, _ we're go - ing to leave you now.

Fare - well, la - dies, _ Fare - well, la - dies, _

Fare - well, la - dies, _ we're go - ing to leave you

now. _

Pick a Little, Talk a Little

Words and Music by Meredith Willson

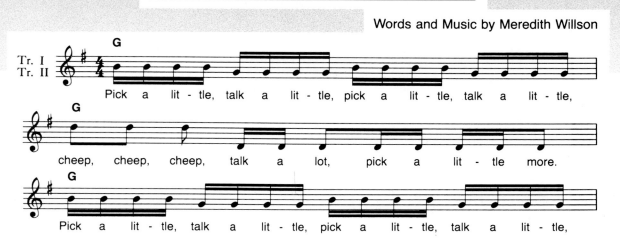

Pick a lit - tle, talk a lit - tle, pick a lit - tle, talk a lit - tle,

cheep, cheep, cheep, talk a lot, pick a lit - tle more.

Pick a lit - tle, talk a lit - tle, pick a lit - tle, talk a lit - tle,

15

Let the Rafters Ring

Words and Music by Dick Smith

The Conductor

A musical performance begins to come alive when the conductor rehearses the performers.

Before the rehearsal, the conductor

- studies the **score** and considers what might contribute to an expressive performance
- makes decisions about **tempo, articulation, dynamics,** and **phrasing**
- prepares the score by adding conducting cues and indicating the performers' entrances and expression markings

During the rehearsal, the conductor directs the performers by

- giving the basic beat pattern with the right hand

 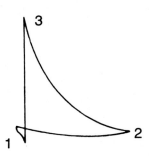 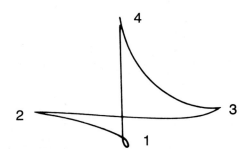

- providing cues for entrances with the left hand

- altering the motions of both hands to communicate expressive ideas

Refer to the score for "Let the Rafters Ring" on pages 16–18. Study the expression markings and the cues shown in red. Practice the basic $\frac{4}{4}$ conducting pattern. Take turns conducting and rehearsing the performers.

The Vocalist

A musical performance often includes vocalists as well as instrumentalists. The vocalists may perform as soloists or as members of an ensemble.

Select the part most appropriate for your range.

Warm up your voice and sing together.

Treble I   Treble II

Changing Voice
(actual pitch)   Baritone

Tr. I
Tr. II

Sing-a-way, sing-a-way, (etc.)

C.V.
Bar.

Sing - a - way, ___ (etc.)

Choose soloists to create improvised melodies. Perform these melodies with the ensemble as they sing "Sing Away . . ."

The Instrumentalist

A musical performance usually includes instrumental performers. They may perform all the parts of the music or provide an accompaniment for the vocalists.

The instrumentalist

- plays the part appropriate for his or her instrument
- practices that part in order to learn the music and play it accurately
- rehearses with the conductor to prepare for the performance

Instrumental parts for "Let the Rafters Ring"

The Choreographer

Many musical performances take on an added dimension when the choreographer creates movements to accompany the music.

The choreographer

- devises interesting movements
- plans a sequence of movements that fits the form of the music
- rehearses the movements with the choir

Create movements for "Let the Rafters Ring." Write down your plan. Rehearse the choreography.

The Arranger

A musical performance may include newly composed songs or arrangements of melodies composed by someone else.

The arranger

- selects an interesting melody
- chooses a musical style
- creates instrumental and vocal parts
- notates a part for each performer

Examine the rhythmic ideas shown below. Listen to the recording of each arrangement and follow the vocal scores beginning on the next page. Can you identify the significant features of each arrangement?

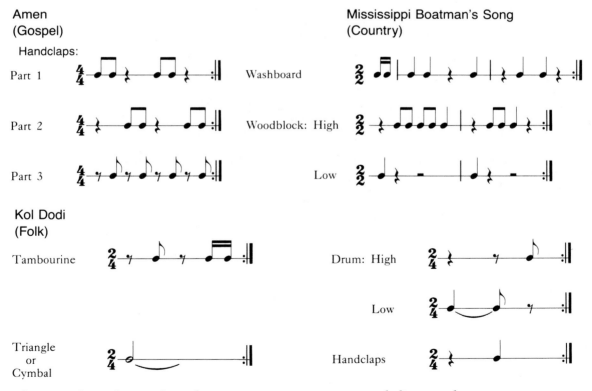

Amen
(Gospel)

Handclaps:

Part 1

Part 2

Part 3

Kol Dodi
(Folk)

Tambourine

Triangle
or
Cymbal

Mississippi Boatman's Song
(Country)

Washboard

Woodblock: High

Low

Drum: High

Low

Handclaps

After you have listened to the various arrangements and discussed the different characteristics of each style, prepare your own arrangement of one of the three songs.

Kol Dodi

Israeli Folk Song

Joyously

Kol do - di, kol do - di, kol do - di, hi - në ze ba.

M'- da- lëg al he - ha - rim, ___ m'- ka- pëts al ___ ha- g'va - ot. ha- g'va - ot.

Mississippi Boatman's Song

Traditional
Arranged by F.W.

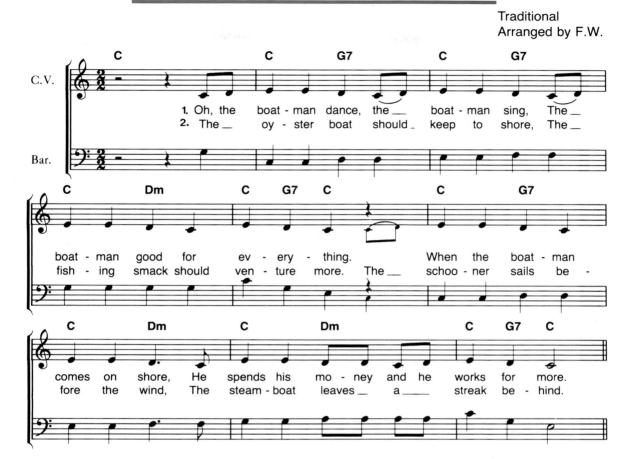

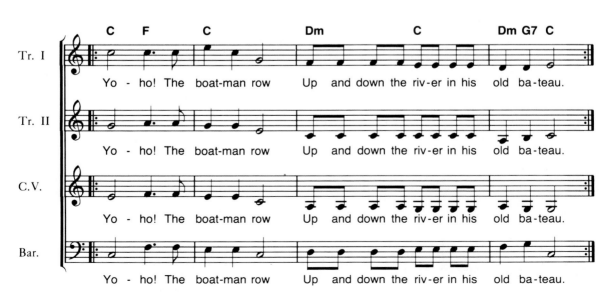

Amen

Spiritual

Arranged by F. W.

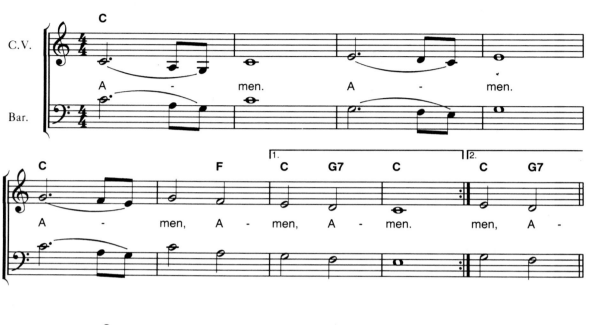

A - men. A - men.

A - men, A - men, A - men. men, A -

1. See the ba - by, Ly - ing in a man - ger.
2. See Him in the tem - ple, Talk - ing to the el - ders, How
3. See Him at the sea - side, Preach - ing and ___ heal - ing,

men. A - men, A -

men. A - men, A -

One Christ - mas morn - ing.
they mar-veled at his wis - dom.
to the blind and the fee - ble.

men, A - men, A - men, A -

men,

Hal - le - lu - jah, In the king - dom

men, A - men, A -

with my Sav - ior. A - men, A - men.

men. A - men, A - men, A - men.

The Television Studio

Television is an important medium for recording and broadcasting

- live concerts
- operas and musicals
- solo recitals
- commentaries about music
- improvised performances
- programs about music
- commercials that use music

How can you use television equipment to assemble a broadcast program that includes a musical performance?

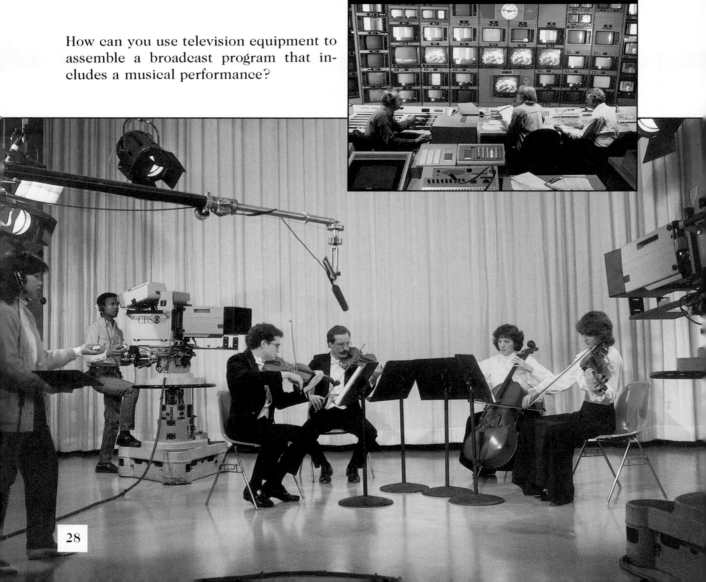

The Production Staff

Personnel	Function	Personnel	Function
Executive Producer	• Is in charge of one or several programs	**Stage Manager**	• Manages all activities on studio floor • Directs performers on the floor, relaying director's cues to the performers and supervising the floor personnel
Producer	• Takes charge of one production • Is responsible for all personnel working on the production • Also, sometimes serves as writer and/or director	**Stage Hands**	• Assemble sets • Display cue cards • Operate other prompting devices • Operate microphone booms
Associate Producer	• Assists producer in all production matters	**Studio or Remote Supervisors**	• Oversee all technical operations
Field Producer	• Assists producer by taking charge of operations away from the studio	**Technical Director**	• Acts as engineering crew chief
Production Assistant	• Assists producer and director	**Camera Operators**	• Operate the cameras
Director	• Is in charge of directing performers and technical crews • Transforms a script into an effective video and audio message	**Lighting Director**	• Controls the lighting of the production
		Video Operators	• Adjust camera controls
		Audio Engineer	• Is in charge of all audio operations
		Videotape Operator	• Runs the videotape machine and does videotape editing

The Television System

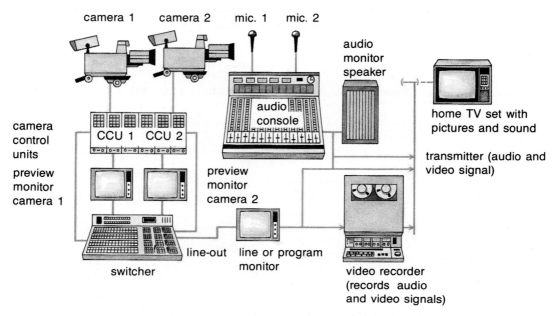

camera 1   camera 2   mic. 1   mic. 2

audio monitor speaker

audio console

camera control units

CCU 1   CCU 2

preview monitor camera 1

preview monitor camera 2

home TV set with pictures and sound

transmitter (audio and video signal)

line-out   line or program monitor

switcher

video recorder (records audio and video signals)

A television system may include very complex equipment, as shown in the diagram above, or it may be quite simple, as shown below. Most school and home equipment will be limited to one camera, one microphone (or a microphone built into the camera), a video recorder, and a monitor or TV set.

Connect your equipment as shown below. A set of headphones should be connected to the headphone or speaker output jack of the recorder.

microphone   camera   headphones   TV set or monitor

video recorder

Planning and Producing A Musical Event

Program *String Quartet*
page *1* of *5*

Video	Audio	Comments
GLENDALE MIDDLE SCHOOL PRESENTS SONG and DANCE —ROBERT WASHBURN	**String Quartet:** (Begin playing at measure 94) (Music ends)	Close camera shot on title card
	Announcer: Welcome to another mini-concert by the Glendale Middle School String Quartet.	Close-up shot of announcer
	Announcer: Today the focus of our concert is 20th century string music, more specifically the music of Robert Washburn.	Begin with shot of announcer; cut to shot of quartet (include all players)
	Announcer: Featured today is first violinist, Darryl White...	Zoom from quartet to first violinist
	Announcer: Second violinist, Sandra Chen...	Pan to second violinist

NOW CASTING!

What Every Singer Should Know About Acting

Needed:

Producer	Chorus and Dancers
Director	Instrumentalists (Pit Orchestra)
Conductor	Costumer
Choreographer	Stage Designer
Singers-Actors:	Rehearsal Pianist
Instructor	Props Manager
Susan	Light and Sound Technicians
George	Publicity Manager

Think about the skills you will need for each role. Decide which on-stage or backstage jobs you might apply for. What criteria should be used in casting these roles?

The Producer

A producer is always available to help and to make sure that all the parts of the production flow smoothly.

The Director

The director may wish to have the actors speak the parts for the first run-through, planning when they are to enter, where they should move, and so on.

The Conductor(s)

The conductors work with the members of the chorus and the orchestra. They prepare the songs and accompaniments, as well as an overture and a finale.

The Vocal Performers

The vocal performers should be able to
- read music
- sing in a style appropriate to the role
- perform expressively
- act the role believably

Prepare for the tryouts. Read the script. Choose one of the roles. Plan how you will perform the role. Think about the melodies you might improvise for your lines.

The Orchestra

Instrumentalists in the orchestra should be able to

- read music
- play an instrument
- improvise or compose a part following a harmonic sequence
- perform expressively
- listen carefully and balance with the rest of the orchestra

Examine this chord sequence. It can be used to accompany "Fame" as sung by the vocal performers (see page 34); repeat this sequence four times and end with the F minor chord.

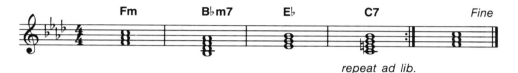

What instruments will you use to play the **root** of each chord? Which instruments will play the remaining pitches? Could someone play a variation of the melody of "Fame" and create an overture? Or new variation for a finale?

Stage Personnel

The stage personnel help to determine production needs, acquire props, and prepare for staging the show.

The Rehearsal

The director and the conductor must work together to plan a smooth transition from the overture to the dramatic action to the closing instrumental finale.

The cast works in groups to prepare the many parts of the production; then the full ensemble premieres the performance.

33

What Every Singer Should Know About Acting

Story by Harvey Rudoff

A fine arts high school in a large metropolitan city. A group of students are in rehearsal, dancing and singing. Their instructor interrupts.

Fame

Lyrics by Dean Pitchford

Music by Michael Gore

Fame! I'm gon-na live for-ev-er. I'm gon-na learn how to fly high! I feel it com-in' to-geth-er. Peo-ple will see me and die. Fame! I'm gon-na make it to hea-ven, Light up the sky like a flame. Fame! I'm gon-na live for-ev-er. Ba-by, re-mem-ber my name, Fame!

Instructor: (*speaking*) Singers are expected to be able to act. Acting lessons are expensive and time-consuming. Many young singers can't afford them. Yet it will do them no good to learn to sing the music if they can't act out the story. What is needed is a jiffy course in acting that contains the basic principles of stagecraft in simple, easily understood terms. Briefly, that is what I propose to do.

We will begin our first lesson by tackling the art of sitting down. (*writes "Sitting Down" on the board to emphasize the point*)

Try sitting down. Go ahead—that's terrible! You need a lot of practice before attempting that before an audience, because sitting down takes place mostly behind you. You can't watch yourself do it. So ask somebody to observe you while you practice, and ask for criticism.

(*Attention is focused on new scene:* Susan practicing sitting.)

Chorus: (*sustains these pitches throughout the improvised recitative*)

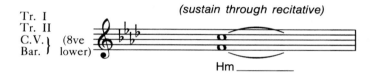

Susan:	Oh, George, come here a minute.
George:	Okay, what do you want?
Susan:	Watch this.
George:	Watch what?
Susan:	This—look. (*sits down*) How was that?
George:	How was what?
Susan:	For heaven's sake, George, I sat down.
George:	Oh.
Susan:	Well?
George:	I guess it was okay.
Susan:	Just "okay"? Is that all you can say?
George:	Well—
Susan:	Look, George, I'll do it again. Now this time, watch. (*sits down again*)
George:	Oh, that's good. That's very good.
Susan:	Thanks, George. (*practices sitting some more*)
George:	Say, that's my lunch you're sitting on!
Susan:	Wha— gee, I'm sorry, George. (*hands him his lunch*)
George:	Thanks.
Susan:	Are you mad, George?
George:	I had a hard-boiled egg and a jelly sandwich in there.

Susan:	I'm sorry, George.
George:	And a tomato.
Susan:	I said I was sorry.
George:	How would you like it if I sat on your lunch?
Susan:	I—
George:	I never did anything to you, did I?
Susan:	Please, George.
George:	If I had known you were going to do that, I wouldn't have put the slice of pie in it.
Susan:	Pie?
George:	I would have put a hard roll in, or an apple, or something that wouldn't squash.
Susan:	Look, George, it was an accident. I didn't mean to sit on your lunch. I was practicing sitting, that's all. I didn't know your lunch was there. Won't you please forgive me, George?
George:	I don't know . . . .
Susan:	I have to practice sitting, George. I want to be an actor, I mean an actress . . . .
George:	An actor? Like Marlon Brando?
Susan:	. . . or someone like Meryl Streep.
George:	I met Marlon Brando once.
Susan:	Really?
George:	He's not the kind of guy that would sit on someone's lunch.
Susan:	Look, George . . . .

(Song returns, sung partway through, with singers humming an accompaniment.)

Fame! I'm gon - na live ___ for - ev - er.

I'm gon - na learn ___ how to fly ___ high!

I feel it com - in' to - geth - er . . .

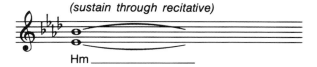

(sustain through recitative)

Hm _____

(Scene briefly shifts back to the instructor.)

Instructor: *(writes on board, "How to Stand Up")* Standing up is not as difficult as sitting down, but to be on the safe side, call someone over and have that person watch you do it.

(Scene changes again to Susan and George.)

Susan: Say, George, come over here and watch me.
George: I'm not talking to you. You sat on my lunch.
Susan: Gosh, are you still thinking about that? That was last week.
George: Well . . . .
Susan: Come on, George, be a good sport and watch me.
George: Well, okay.
Susan: How do I look? *(stands up)*
George: Fine—except the way you're standing.
Susan: What's wrong with how I'm standing?
George: Oh, never mind. It's nothing.
Susan: I want to know, George. Tell me.
George: Forget it. I'd better not.
Susan: Please tell me. How else will I become a good actor?
George: Well, if you must know—you're standing on my lunch.

(Chorus sings first three phrases of "Fame" as scene shifts back to the classroom)

Instructor: *(writes on board, "Today's Lesson: How to Cry")* In order to cry, you must think of something really sad. Think of the dent you put in the front fender of your dad's car.

It is true that some actors conceal half an onion in a pocket as they go onstage. When they have to cry, they take a whiff of it and burst into tears. The trouble is that any onion strong enough to make you cry can also be smelled by the people in the first six rows of the theater. It is embarrassing to see them cry before you do. In short, you must have a good reason to cry. It is better not to fake it. Now take that young man over there. See him? Listen to those sobs! His face is buried in his hands, and his shoulders are heaving in absolute grief. I can see the tears dropping to the floor, can't you? That young man must certainly have something to cry about. Why, isn't that George? Oh, for Pete's sake, George!

(Curtain descends as the chorus sings the complete song "Fame.")

Big River

Words and Music by Roger Miller

Cast: (Main Characters)

Mark Twain, *the author*
Huckleberry Finn, *motherless boy*
The Widow Douglas, *Tom's guardian*
Jim, *runaway slave*
Miss Watson, *owner of Jim*
Tom Sawyer, *Huck's friend*
The King, *con artist*
The Duke, *con artist*
Mary Jane Wilkes, *Huck's sweetheart*
Pap Finn, *Huck's father*

The Setting: *Along the Mississippi River in the late 1800s*
The Story: *A musical adaptation of Mark Twain's adventure story "Huckleberry Finn"*

Overture (excerpt)

Act I

The scene opens with what seems to be all the townspeople of Petersburg telling Huck who he should be and how he should act. Everyone lectures him about learning to read and write and warns against being a loafer:

> Hey, hey, ain't the situation concernin' education aggravatin'? And how!
> Do you wanna get to heaven?
> Well, you'd better get your lessons or you won't know how . . .

Later that night Huck sneaks out of his bedroom to join Tom Sawyer and other friends in the cave. They brag about all the mischief they'll do in town. After a while Huck returns home.

Later that night Huck's Pap shows up in Huck's bedroom and drags his son off to a cabin in the woods. He threatens and yells at Huck. When his Pap is asleep, Huck sees the chance to escape. He runs away to hide on Jackson's Island. While on the island he reflects on his character, singing a plaintive song.

Waitin' for the Light to Shine

I have lived in the dark-ness for so long, I'm wait-ing for the light to shine. Far be-yond ho-ri-zons, I have seen be-yond the things I've been, be-yond the dreams I've dreamed, are the things I've done, In fact each and ev-ery one are the way that I was taught to run. I am wait-ing for the light to shine, I am wait-ing for the light to shine. I have lived in the dark-ness for so long, I'm wait-ing for the light to shine.

Huck's reflective mood doesn't last long. The free-spirited Huck bounces back by showing his "I don't care" attitude:

> I, Huckleberry, me
> Hereby declare myself to be
> Nothing ever other than
> Exactly what I am . . .

Huck soon finds that he is not alone on Jackson's Island. Miss Watson's slave Jim, who has run away to keep from being sold downriver in New Orleans, is also there. Huck makes a decision to team up with Jim and help him to get to the free states. With just minutes to spare, they evade a posse by shoving a raft onto the river. Then they head away for freedom.

Muddy Water

Refrain
Look out for me, oh, mud-dy wa-ter, your mys-ter-ies are deep and wide,_ And I got a need for go-in' some-place, and I_ got a need to climb_ up on your back and ride. _____ Fine

Verses
1. You can look for
2. Well _ I've been

me / down when you see me com-in'. / to the pain and sor-row I may be run-nin', I don't / Of no to-mor-rows com-in'

know. / in, I may be tired _____ and run-nin' fe-ver, / But I put my pole _____ to the riv-er bot-tom, But I'll _ be / And I _ got-ta

(Refrain) D.S. al Fine
head-in' south _ for the mouth of the O-hi-o. }
hide some-place _ to _ find my-self a-gain. }

So look out for

42

The road to freedom is hazardous. Huck and Jim narrowly escape capture and a collision with a steamboat. When all finally seems quiet, they are interrupted by a couple of con artists, King and Duke, who are trying to escape an angry mob. King and Duke commandeer the raft with Huck and Jim still on it. Once they are safely away from the mob, they begin to sing about how they duped the townsfolk. Huck is drawn into their talk and joins their singing.

When the Sun Goes Down in the South

Verse 1:
When the sun goes down in the south
And the moon comes up in the east,
Well, step right up and see the wonder of the ages.
It's a guaranteed visual feast.

Refrain:
When the darkness falls on the town
And the north star's startin' to rise
Oh, you can't imagine a menagerie air
Created by a couple of guys.

Verse 2:
Well, anybody wonderin' what they're going to see
Is gonna have to ante up a dollar for the ticket.
Anybody wonderin' what's goin' on
Is gonna find out when they chase us through the thicket.

(repeat Refrain)

Verse 3:
When the sun goes down in the south
And the hayseeds stand in line.
Well, step right up and see the duo
Bod'ly do the doo wah diddy on the clothes line.

Act II

The second act begins with King, Duke, and Huck going ashore at Bricktown, Arkansas to con the townsfolk while Jim remains with the raft. They are delighted when an unsuspecting "young fool" brags about a fortune left by a death in the Wilkes family. King and Duke present themselves as the rightful heirs to the fortune, depriving the beautiful and innocent Mary Jane Wilkes of her estate. Huck, smitten with Mary Jane, steals the money back. When Huck is trying to return the money to Mary Jane's home, she appears unexpectedly. Mary Jane sings an ironic love song to her dear departed father. Huck listens as he hides nearby.

You Oughta Be Here with Me

If you think it's lonesome where you are tonight,
Then you oughta be here with me.
If you think there's heartaches where you are tonight,
Then you oughta be here with me.
'Cause with you I'm whole, without you I'm cold.
If teardrops are fallin' where you are tonight,
Then you oughta be here with me.
Is loneliness callin' where you are tonight?
Then you oughta be here with me.
'Cause with you I'm whole, without you I'm cold.
So if you think about me where you are tonight,
Then you oughta be here with me.

Upon finding out what Huck has done for her, Mary Jane asks him to stay awhile and become her friend. He is deeply moved but also realizes his responsibility to Jim. The conflict of indecision is reflected in the song Huck, Mary Jane, and Jim sing. (*Two scenes are shown, one depicting Mary Jane and Huck in town and the other showing Jim at the river.*)

Leavin's Not the Only Way to Go

Did the morn-ing come too ear - ly? Was the
lay and let your feel - ings grow ac -

night not long e - nough?_ Does a tear of hes - i - ta - tion fall____ on
cus-tomed to the dark _ And by morn-ing's light you just _ might solve __ the

ev - ery-thing you touch? Well, it might be just a les - son for the
prob-lems of the heart. And it all might be a les - son for the

has - ty heart to know. _ May-be leav-in's not the on - ly way _ to go. _
has - ty heart to know. _ May-be leav-in's not the on - ly way _ to go. _

_ 2. May-be _ Peo-ple reach new _ un-der-stand - ings all_the

time. They take a sec-ond look, may-be change their mind. Peo-ple

reach new _ un-der-stand - ings ev - ery day. ____ Tell me not to

reach, I'll just go a - way.＿ Did the morn-ing come too ear-ly? Was the

night not long e - nough?＿ Does a tear of hes - i - ta - tion fall ＿ on

ev-ery-thing＿ you touch? Well, it might be just a les - son for the

has - ty heart to know,＿ May-be leav-in's not the on - ly way＿ to go. ＿

＿ And a heart with-out ＿ a home ＿ is such a

lone-ly row to hoe. May-be leav-in's not the on - ly way＿ to go. ＿＿

Huck returns to the raft, only to find that Duke has been tarred and feathered and Jim is gone. Duke admits he has sold Jim. Huck feels guilty and writes to Miss Watson, telling her where she can find Jim. Feeling even more depressed, he tears up the letter, determined to free Jim by himself. In a surprising turn to the plot, Tom Sawyer shows up and decides to help Huck free Jim from his captors. Huck and Tom succeed in freeing Jim. Jim gets ready to go up North to make money and free his family. Huck decides to go out West to get away from any attempts to "civilize" him. Huck and Jim sing a reprise of "Muddy Water," and Tom and Huck part with Jim as he heads up the river.

Huck ends up alone once more, thinking of their journey. "It was like the fortune Jim predicted long ago," he says, "consider-able trouble and considerable joy."

The Critic

A musical performance may seem to end with the final curtain, but for the performers there is one more important moment: when they open the morning papers to read the review prepared by the critic.

Music Notes *by Anne Welsbacher*

The Farnsworth Falls Youth Symphony, consisting of senior high school students, gave an even and solid performance of Smetana's "The Moldau" and Borodin's *Symphony No. 2 in B minor*. The first piece, conducted by Sheila Halpern, opened well, with a flute solo that flowed smoothly and was strong without being overbearing. Although the woodwind section had some difficulty with pitch—especially the English horn, which was often flat—the piece as a whole was played well, with knowledge of the material evident, particularly in the string section. Conductor Halpern paced the composition well, with particularly fine control over the final climactic tempo. The piece by Borodin was the better performed of the two; conductor John Ricardo kept the majesty intact and a steady, strong rhythm prevailed throughout. The string section gave a particularly fine rendition of the opening measures of the composition; the strings were perfectly on pitch and set a tempo from which the orchestra as an ensemble never wavered. Both pieces were well balanced; the winds never covered the strings, and the accompaniment was delicate while providing a solid foundation for the main theme.

Analyze these two newspaper reviews.

Make a list of the aspects of the performance that the reviewer discusses.

Collect reviews of musical performances from a newspaper or magazine. Do your samples touch on the same topics as the reviews shown here?

Attend a local concert or performance of a musical, and write a review.

Oklahoma! by Rodgers and Hammerstein was produced with vitality and warmth by the Farnsworth State University Theater last weekend. The musical takes place in Oklahoma, shortly before it becomes a state of the Union, and deals with two sets of sweethearts, their families and friends. Pat Brooks, as Laurie, played her role with honesty and vigor. She gave her character personality, singing her love songs with the same good timing and high quality that she shows when she speaks. Barbara Mason, as the comic character Ado Annie, had tremendous energy, and Carol Shapiro, as the kind, no-nonsense Aunt Eller, gave strength to the musical. Also good were Brad Davis as Curly and Greg Murphy as Will. Tom Sonno, as the "heavy," Jud, succeeded in creating the moody character, and his "In My Room" was chilling and effective. The orchestra, directed by Elspeth Esterhazy, was professional and talented; the effective lighting was by Jo-Ann Corelli; the fine costumes by John Franklin; and the well-paced direction by Cindy Stewart.

The Record Collector

The big performance is over. The reviews have been written; the performers have continued their tour to another town. You can still remember the music . . . sort of. With a recording, you can have the performance, or one like it, at your fingertips.

The Record Collector

- sometimes goes shopping for a specific recording by a specific performer
- sometimes browses through the bins of the local record shop to discover recordings of all kinds of music
- sometimes goes to the public library to compare two performances of the same composition before purchasing a recording of one performance
- always takes good care of records (and tapes) to preserve their quality

Always pick up a record by the edges; never allowing your hands to touch it. Keep records free of lint. You may want to purchase a special cleaning cloth. Be sure that the record player needle is in good condition, or that the tape heads on the tape deck are clean. When placing the needle on a record, take care not to scrape it across the record; always put the needle down slowly and carefully.

LISTENING

The Great Gate of Kiev
from *Pictures at an Exhibition*
by Modest Mussorgsky

Modest Mussorgsky (1839–1881) was a Russian composer of the Romantic era. Among his best-known works are "A Night on Bald Mountain" and the opera *Boris Godunov.*

Listen to four different recordings of this music. How would you prepare information about each version for use by a record collector?

When I'm on My Journey

Afro-American Song

Verse **C**

1. When I'm on my jour - ney, don't you weep af - ter me.

G   **G7**   **C**

When I'm on my jour - ney, don't you weep af - ter me.

C   **C7**   **F**   *Refrain*

When I'm on my jour - ney, don't you weep af - ter me. I don't

C   **G7**   **C**

want you to weep af - ter me.

2. High upon the mountain, leave your troubles down below. (*3 times*)
   (*Refrain*)

3. When the stars are falling and the thunder starts to roll. (*3 times*)
   (*Refrain*)

4. Every lonely river must go home to the sea. (*3 times*)
   (*Refrain*)

Unit 2

The Listening Experience

Listening to Music

We can listen to music
- in the concert hall
- on recordings
- on the radio
- on television
- during a dance performance

Listening to music is like entering a time machine. We can be carried instantly out of our surroundings to any point in history.
We can

- enter a medieval monastery at evensong
- dance on the village green in merry old England
- join the town choir as Bach prepares a new chorale
- seat ourselves in a concert hall in Vienna, dressed in our gowns or tail coats and powdered wigs

Each generation has left behind a living music that says to us: This is how we thought . . . how we lived . . . who we were.
Listen carefully! Our music is part of you.
You will hear us in the sounds of your orchestras.
You will hear us in the melodies of your songs.
You will hear us, for we are still with you today.
Explore the music of past generations, for it is very much a part of today's music.
Listen to several musical examples from various periods of history. Can you guess when each selection was composed?

Look at the time line on the next few pages. Learn about people and events, and look at works of art from each era. Listen again to the musical compositions. Try to connect each musical example with the era in which it was written.

A Time Line

The Medieval Era (800-1450)

Viking explorers reach North America (c. 1000).
William of Normandy conquers England (1066).
The Magna Carta, an early constitution, is written in England (1215).
The Venetian merchant and explorer Marco Polo travels in China (1275-1292).
Christians set out on Crusades (11th-14th centuries).

Composers:
Guillaume de Machaut (1300-1377),
Francesco Landini (1325-1397),
Guillaume Dufay (c. 1400-1474)

The Renaissance (1450-1600)

Christopher Columbus arrives in North America (1492).
The Protestant Reformation begins (1517).
Ships commanded by Ferdinand Magellan sail around the world (1519-1522).
William Shakespeare is active as a playwright in England (1564-1616).

Composers:
Josquin des Prez (1450-1521),
Thomas Tallis (c. 1505-1585),
Giovanni Palestrina (1525-1594)

The Baroque Era (1600-1750)

The Pilgrims found Plymouth Colony (1620).
Robert de La Salle claims the Louisiana territory for France (1682).
Sir Isaac Newton discovers the law of gravity (1687).
The Industrial Revolution begins in England (1700's).

Composers:
Claudio Monteverdi (1567-1643),
Johann Sebastian Bach (1685-1750),
George Frederick Handel (1685-1759)

The Classical Era (1750-1825)

The French and Indian War is fought in North America (1754-1763).
The Declaration of Independence is written (1776).
The American colonies become an independent nation after winning the Revolutionary War (1775-1783).
The French Revolution begins (1789).

Composers:
Franz Joseph Haydn (1732-1809),
Wolfgang Amadeus Mozart (1756-1791),
Ludwig van Beethoven (1770-1827)

The Romantic Era (1825-1900)

Napoleon is crowned emperor (1804).
The United States and Britain fight the war of 1812 (1812-1815).
Mexican independence is declared (1821).
The California Gold Rush takes place (1848).
The Civil War is fought in the United States (1861-1865).
The telegraph, electric lightbulb, and telephone are invented.

Composers:
Hector Berlioz (1803-1869),
Robert Schumann (1810-1856),
Richard Wagner (1813-1883),
Johannes Brahms (1833-1897)

The Early Twentieth Century (1900-1950)

The Wright brothers fly the first airplane (1903).
Albert Einstein publishes his theory of relativity (1905).
The Bolshevik Revolution takes place in Russia (1917).
World Wars I and II are fought (1914-1918 and 1939-1945).
The United Nations is founded (1946).
Atomic power is developed.
The automobile, radio, sound movies, and television are invented.

Composers:
Claude Debussy (1862-1918),
Arnold Schoenberg (1874-1951),
Igor Stravinsky (1882-1971),
Aaron Copland (1900-   )

Later Twentieth Century (1950-present)

The age of the computer begins (1950).
The United States is involved in wars in Korea (1950-1953) and Vietnam (1964-1975).
The first earth satellite is launched by the Soviets (1957).
The United States lands astronauts on the moon (1969).

Composers:
Elliot Carter (1908-   ),
Luciano Berio (1925-   ),
Pauline Oliveros (1932-   ),
John Cage (1912-   ),
Ellen Zwilich (1939-   ),
Milton Babbitt (1916-   )

55

Clues to Musical Style: Instrumental Timbre

As you listen to music of different times, you may notice differences that are related to the sound of the instruments. Listen to the instruments pictured here. Compare the sounds of old and new. Describe the differences. Is the sound thin and straight or rich and full with little or much resonance?

Notice the expressiveness of the sound. Is there much contrast in the use of dynamics, tempo, articulation, and phrasing?

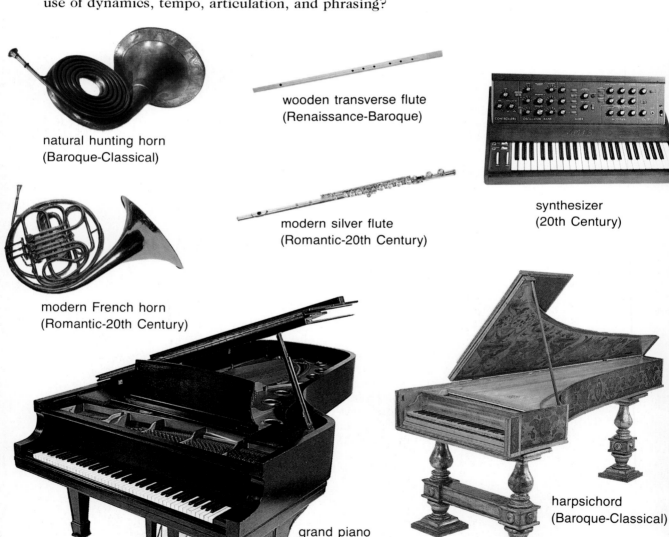

natural hunting horn
(Baroque-Classical)

wooden transverse flute
(Renaissance-Baroque)

synthesizer
(20th Century)

modern French horn
(Romantic-20th Century)

modern silver flute
(Romantic-20th Century)

grand piano
(Romantic-20th Century)

harpsichord
(Baroque-Classical)

The number and types of timbres that are combined influence the quality of sound and help us identify the period in which the music was composed.

Listen: can you identify which groups of instruments are playing and which period the music is from?

Prelude to Act III from *Lohengrin*

by Richard Wagner

Richard Wagner (1813–1883) was one of the most important composers of the Romantic era. Wagner devoted most of his life to composing operas. He regarded opera as a total art work encompassing music, drama, and visual art. Wagner's opera *Lohengrin* is representative of certain aspects of music from the Romantic era. The large symphony orchestra featuring many contrasting timbres is the hallmark of the late nineteenth century. The prominent use of **brass** and **percussion** instruments, the chromatic melodic lines set in very high registers, and the dramatic climaxes add to the emotional quality of this truly romantic music.

1. The prelude opens with the vigorous "Festival Theme," played *fortissimo* by the entire orchestra and punctuated by crashes of cymbals. Notice the **chromatic** nature of the melody. The "Festival Theme" is stated twice.

2. The **tone color** of the French horns makes the introduction of the "March Theme" especially imposing.

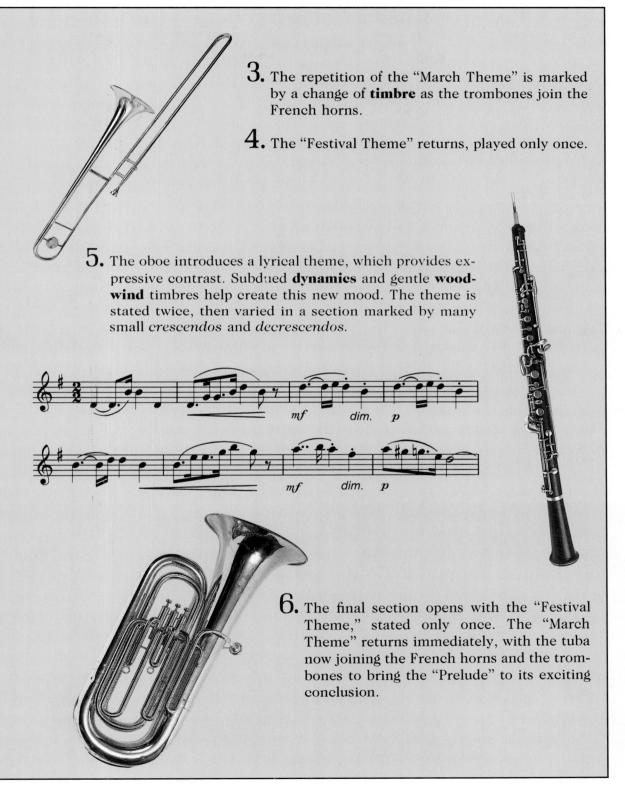

3. The repetition of the "March Theme" is marked by a change of **timbre** as the trombones join the French horns.

4. The "Festival Theme" returns, played only once.

5. The oboe introduces a lyrical theme, which provides expressive contrast. Subdued **dynamics** and gentle **woodwind** timbres help create this new mood. The theme is stated twice, then varied in a section marked by many small *crescendos* and *decrescendos*.

6. The final section opens with the "Festival Theme," stated only once. The "March Theme" returns immediately, with the tuba now joining the French horns and the trombones to bring the "Prelude" to its exciting conclusion.

Clues to Musical Style: Vocal Timbre

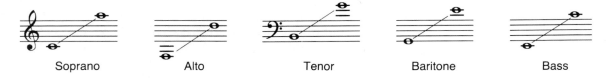

As you hear vocal music from various periods in history, you may find clues that are similar to the ones you noticed in instrumental music.

Listen to vocal music from the Medieval era and from the Twentieth century. As you listen carefully to each example, consider these characteristics:

The source of the sound

| Soprano | Alto | Tenor | Baritone | Bass |

The quality of the sound

> Is the sound rich and full? Does the singer use **vibrato?** Is the vibrato full or limited?

The expressiveness of the sound

> Is there much contrast in the use of dynamics, tempo, articulation, and phrasing?

The vocal style used by a singer is often influenced by the origin and style of the music. A sensitive performer may alter the vocal quality and the expressiveness of the sound to reflect the style of music being sung.

"*Nacht*" (Night) from *Pierrot Lunaire*, Opus 21

by Arnold Schoenberg

Arnold Schoenberg (1874–1951) was a major figure in Twentieth century music. He wrote for many kinds of instrumental and vocal ensembles and was an influential teacher, author, and painter, as well as a composer.

This composition for voice and chamber ensemble, first performed in 1912, introduced a new form of singing called *sprechgesang*. After you have listened, try to develop your own definition of this German word.

> Sinister giant black butterflies
> Shrouded the sun's bright rays.
> Like a sealed book of magic spells,
> The horizon rests . . . in silence.

Reverberation

Experiment with your own *sprechgesang*.

Use the ideas you gained while listening to "Night."
The following score may serve as a guide.

Solo Voice: Crossing it alone
In cold moonlight . . .
The brittle bridge
Echoes my footsteps.
Tagai

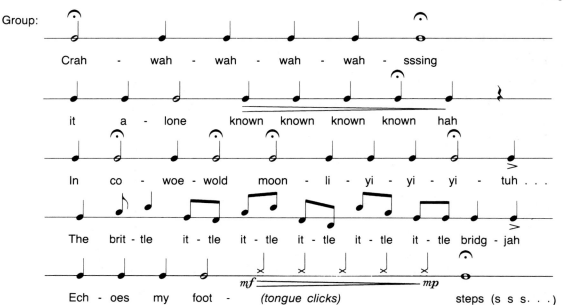

Group:

Crah - wah - wah - wah - wah - sssing

it a - lone known known known known hah

In co - woe - wold moon - li - yi - yi - yi - tuh . . .

The brit - tle it - tle it - tle it - tle it - tle it - tle bridg - jah

Ech - oes my foot - (tongue clicks) steps (s s s . . .)

mf ———— *mp*

Clues to Musical Style: Rhythm

When we listen to music of different periods, we may first notice the different sounds of instruments and voices. Next we may notice differences in the way rhythm is organized. Listen to a

- religious chant from the Medieval era
- pavane from the Renaissance
- minuet from the Classical period
- twentieth-century vocal work with instruments

As you listen to each piece, notice how rhythmic characteristics are used:

Does the underlying beat occur at

- regular intervals?

- irregular intervals?

Do **accents** occur

- regularly?

- irregularly?

Is the beat strongly heard or almost absent?

Does the flow of the rhythmic line move

- in even, regular patterns in relation to the underlying beat?

━━ ▬ ▬ ━━ ━━ ▬ ▬ ▬ ▬ ▬ ▬ ━━━
▬ ▬ ▬ ▬ ▬ ▬ ▬ ▬ ▬ ▬ ▬ ▬ ▬

- freely, with no recurring beats?

━━ ▬ ▬ ━━ ━━ ▬ ━━ ▬▬ ━━ • • • • ━━
▬ ▬ ▬ ▬ ▬ ▬ ▬ ▬ ▬ ▬ ▬

Do the rhythmic lines interweave by moving

- in even relationships to each other and to the beat?

━━━ ━━━ ━━━ ━━━ ━━━ ▬▬ ▬▬ ▬▬ ━━━
▬ ▬ ▬ ▬ ▬ ▬ ▬ ▬ ▬ ▬ ▬

- unevenly, as though unrelated to each other?

━━━ ▬ ━━ ▬▬ ━━ ━━ ▬ ▬ ▬▬ ━━ ▬▬ ▬
━━ ━━ ━━ ▬▬ ━━━ ━━ ━━ ▬ ━━ ▬ ▬▬ ━━ ▬

- in mixed fashion, with some even and some uneven rhythmic lines?

━━━ ━━ ▬ ▬▬ ━━ ━━ ▬▬ ▬▬ ━━ ▬▬ ▬
━━ ━━ ━━ ▬▬ ━━━ ━━ ▬ ━━ ▬ ━━ ▬

━━━ ▬ ━━ ▬ ━━ ━━ ▬ ▬▬ ━━ ▬▬ ━━
▬ ━━ ▬ ━━ ━━ ━━ ▬ ━━ ▬ ━━

Rhythm and Dance

One of the important influences on the musical style of a society is its dance forms. As nearly as we can tell, the earliest instrumental music was developed as an accompaniment to the dance. Dance accompaniment continues to be an important function of social music.

Listen to dance music of four different eras. Learn each dance. Discuss ways in which

- the dance steps reflect the rhythms in the music
- the form of the dance reflects the musical form

In the Renaissance Era:
The Pavane
Belle qui tiens ma vie by Thoinot Arbeau
Thoinot Arbeau (1519–1595) was a French composer of dance music. Arbeau was also an author and wrote instructions for the dances of his time.

In the Classical Era:
The Minuet
"Menuetto" from *Don Giovanni* by Wolfgang Amadeus Mozart
Wolfgang Amadeus Mozart (1756–1791) is considered by many to be one of the greatest composers that ever lived. This minuet is from one of his many operas. Mozart also composed a large body of solo keyboard pieces, instrumental sonatas, music for various chamber ensembles, and sacred music for chorus and orchestra.

**In the Romantic Era:
The Waltz**
The Emperor Waltz
by Johann Strauss, Jr.
Johann Strauss, Jr. (1825–
1899) was a Viennese com-
poser known for his waltzes
and operettas. Strauss was
very popular in his lifetime
and was referred to as "the
king of the waltz."

**In the Twentieth Century:
The Charleston**
Twelfth-Street Rag
by Euclay L. Bowman
The Charleston was a dance
of the 1920s, probably named
after the city in South Carolina. Bowman (1887–1949)
was one of many composers
at this time who wrote popular music for dance.

Clues to Musical Style: Melody

Next to rhythm, the most important and interesting musical element is probably **melody**. You discovered that rhythmic organization may sometimes be a clue to the musical style. The way a melody is organized may also help you identify its historical period. Listen to a melody. As you listen, try drawing its shape. Could the contour you drew be described as

undulating?   arched?   terraced?   irregular or   ?

Another characteristic of melody is **range**.

Listen again. Does the distance between the highest and lowest pitches seem to be

very wide?   moderate?   very narrow?

A melody may also be described as having **motion**.

As you listen a third time, think about the distance between the individual pitches. Did the melody usually move by

skips?   steps?   a combination of both?

In many melodies, the pitches will often move in relation to a **central pitch.** Draw a line across your sheet of paper to represent the central pitch (the pitch to which all other pitches seem to return in a given key). Then draw the contour of the melody as you listen again. Show the melody as it moves above, moves below, and returns to that central pitch.

Does it seem to return frequently to the central pitch?

central pitch

Or does no one pitch seem to be more important than another?

central pitch

By listening carefully to music of various periods, you may be able to describe some differences in the way melodies are organized.

Listen to and compare the melodies of

- The Renaissance
- The Romantic era
- The Classical period
- The Twentieth century

Clues to Musical Style: Texture

For nearly a thousand years, music of the Western tradition has been composed of several lines moving in relation to each other, not of just a single melodic line.

The relationship of these lines can be a clue to the historical period of the music.

Can you define these three different types of **texture** just by looking at musical examples?

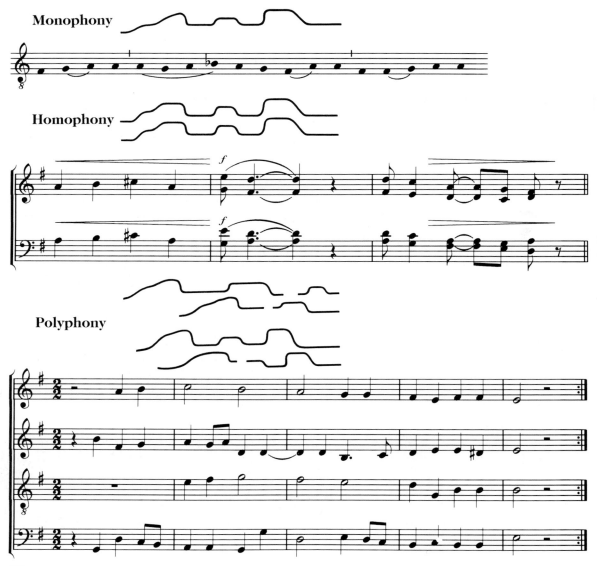

Procession (Hodie Christus Natus Est) from A Ceremony of Carols

Music by Benjamin Britten

Benjamin Britten (1913–1976) was a prominent English composer of this century. The Gregorian chant, *Hodie Christus Natus Est*, was used by Britten in his composition, *A Ceremony of Carols*. The "Procession" is based on church music from the Medieval era.

Morning Has Broken

Words by Eleanor Farjeon

Gaelic Melody
Arranged by Buryl Red

Perform this composition in a homophonic style by

- singing the melody in unison with piano accompaniment
- performing it as a four-part hymn

Listen to a contemporary performance of this melody. Is it still in a homophonic style?

1. Morn - ing has bro - ken Like the first morn - ing, Black-bird has spo - ken Like the first
2. Sweet the rain's new fall Sun - lit from heav - en, Like the first dew - fall On the first
3. Mine is the sun - light; Mine is the morn - ing Born of the one light E - den saw

oh ___

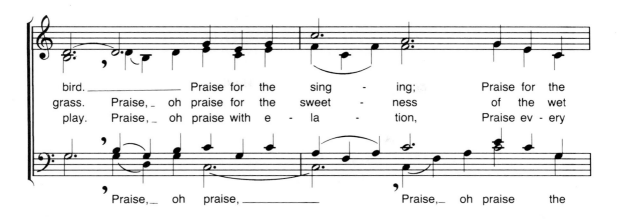

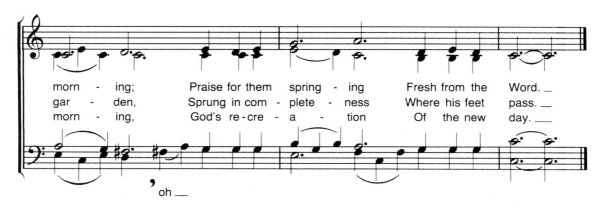

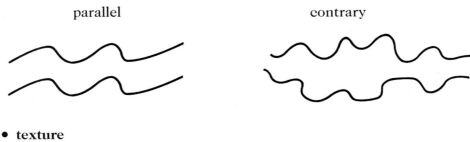

bird. _____ Praise for the sing - ing; Praise for the
grass. Praise, _ oh praise for the sweet - ness of the wet
play. Praise, _ oh praise with e - la - tion, Praise ev - ery

Praise, _ oh praise, _____ Praise, _ oh praise the

morn - ing; Praise for them spring - ing Fresh from the Word. _
gar - den, Sprung in com - plete - ness Where his feet pass. _
morn - ing, God's re - cre - a - tion Of the new day. _

oh _

Can you identify homophonic, monophonic, and polyphonic textures just by listening? Notice other characteristics of texture:

- **the number of lines**

- **motion**

  parallel   contrary

- **texture**

  thick   thin

So Ben Mi Ch'a Bon Tempo

Words of unknown authorship

Music by Orazio Vecchi

Orazio Vecchi (1550–1605) was an Italian composer and poet of the Renaissance. He composed both sacred music for the church and secular music for patrons of the nobility.

Translation: I know well who is happy,
But I will not say.
I know well who is favored,
Alas, I cannot say.
Oh, if only I could say
Who goes, who stays, who comes.

2. *So ben ch'è favorito, so ben ch'è favorito,*
   Fa la la la . . .
   Ahimè no'l posso dir, ahimè no'l posso dir,
   Fa la la la . . .

3. *O s'io potessi dire, o s'io potessi dire,*
   Fa la la la . . .
   Chi va, chi sta, chi vien, chi va, chi sta, chi vien,
   Fa la la la . . .

Music and Drama

Music has been an important part of the theater for hundreds of years. From **miracle plays** to **opera** to **Broadway musicals**, creators of drama have turned to music to help tell story, create a mood, and convey the feelings of characters in their stories.

Whether the composer was a medieval monk in a monastery or is a contemporary artist writing for television, some musical devices used to express dramatic ideas have remained the same.

In this chapter you will

- describe the differences in musical theater of various times and places
- identify characteristics of musical theater
- participate in informal dramatizations of musical theater

Review . . .   *Big River*—a Broadway musical of the eighties

Listen to . . .   *The Play of Daniel*—a miracle play of the 12th century

Madama Butterfly—an opera composed at the turn of this century

The Tender Land—an American folk opera of the 1950s

Compare . . .   the ways music helps to tell the story, create a mood, convey feelings

Begin . . .   by listening to an overture from a Broadway musical. How does this overture help set the scene? create mood? identify characters? predict plot?

The Play of Daniel

Musical drama has been popular for centuries. This play is nearly eight hundred years old. It was probably first performed in one of the medieval cathedrals of France. The music combines characteristics of religious and secular music of the time.

Ductia

Although the music heard on the recording was not part of the original play, music of this type probably accompanied sections of the drama. Listen for each of these medieval instruments.

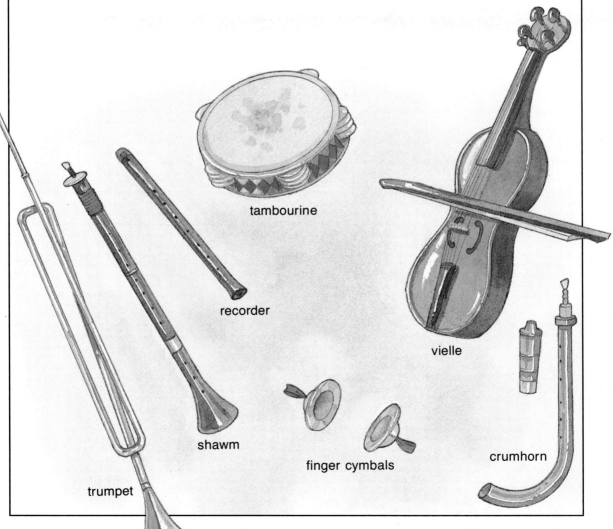

tambourine

recorder

vielle

shawm

finger cymbals

crumhorn

trumpet

75

Long Live the King (Fanfare)

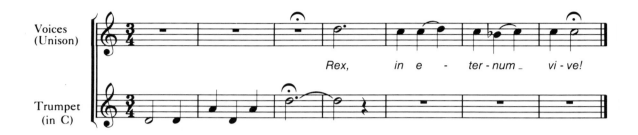

Let Us All Give Thanks Together

Recorder (soprano or alto): Play Treble I part.
Triangle, small and large drums, and finger cymbals: Play stems up on the percussion part below.

Tambourine: Play stems down.

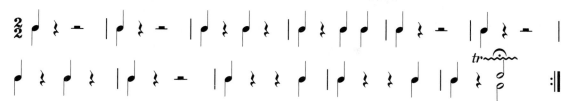

Metallophone:

Cast

King Belshazzar, *king of Babylon*   **Counselors**
Satraps, *noble lords*   **Soldiers**
Queen   **Princes**
Daniel, *a Jewish prophet*   **Musicians**
King Darius, *the new king*   **Angels**
Habakkuk, *a Jewish prophet*

The play opens as the king, Belshazzar, ascends his throne while the Satraps sing and bring forth vessels stolen from the Temple of the Jews.

Satraps:

Jubilemus Regi nostro
   magno ac potenti!
Resonemus laude digna
   voce competenti!

Resonet jocunda turba
   solemnibus odis!
Cytharizent, plaudant manus,
   mille sonent modis!

Pater ejus destruens
   Judaeorum templa,
Magna fecit, et hic regnat
   ejus per exempla.

Pater ejus spoliavit
   regnum Judaeorum;
Hic exaltat sua festa
   decore vasorum.

Let us praise our King,
   great and powerful!
Let us resound with worthy praise
   and fitting song!

Let the merry throng break forth
   in solemn chants;
Let them play their harps, clap their hands,
   sing a thousand tunes.

His father destroyed
   the Temple of the Jews,
And now this one reigns
   by his father's example.

His father took great booty
   from the kingdom of the Jews;
Now he can make his feasts more splendid
   with such handsome vessels.

Haec sunt vasa regia
    quibus spoliatur
Jerusalem, et regalis
    Babylon ditatur.
	These are the royal vessels
	    which were taken
	From Jerusalem, and now adorn
	    regal Babylon.

Ridens plaudit Babylon,
    Jerusalem plorat;
Haec orbatur, haec triumphans
    Belshazzar adorat.
	With laughter, Babylon rejoices;
	    Jerusalem weeps.
	She has been deprived of her children,
	    while Babylon in triumph venerates
	    King Belshazzar.

Omnes ergo exultemus
    tantae potestati
Offerentes Regis vasa
    suae majestati.
	Therefore, let everyone rejoice
	    at such great power,
	Offering these royal vessels
	    to his majesty.

Suddenly, a hand appears and writes on the wall:
    Mane, Thechel, Phares.
The king is in terror and assures the court that anyone knowing the meaning of these words will be given power over Babylon, but his wise men are of no help.

The queen enters and suggests that Daniel, a captured prophet of the Jews, might be able to interpret the words. The soldiers bring Daniel before Belshazzar.

Daniel:	Rex, in eternum vive!	Long live the King!

Belshazzar:	Tune Daniel nomine diceris,
	Huc adductus cum Judaeae
	    miseris?
	Dicunt te habere Dei spiritum
	Et praescire quodlibet
	    absconditum.
	Si ergo potes scripturam
	    solvere,
	Immensis muneribus ditabere.
		Are you not called Daniel,
		Brought here with the wretches of Judea?
		They say you have the spirit of God
		And foresee whatever is hidden.
		If then you can solve this writing,
		You will be enriched with countless gifts.

Daniel:

Rex, tua nolo munera;	O King, I wish not your gifts;
Gratis solvetur litera.	Unrewarded I will solve the letters.
Est autem haec solutio:	This is the solution:
Instat tibi confusio.	Affliction awaits you.
Pater tuus prae omnibus	Your father above all others
Potens olim potentibus,	Once was powerful.
Turgens nimis superbia	Swollen with excessive pride
Dejectus est a gloria	He was cast down from glory.
Et Mane, dicit Dominus,	For *Mane,* says the Lord,
Est tui regni terminus.	Is the end of your kingdom;
Thechel libram significat	*Thechel* means a measuring weight,
Quae te minorem indicat.	Which means you are weaker;
Phares, hoc est divisio,	*Phares,* that is division,
Regnum transportat alio.	Your kingdom will be given to another.

Belshazzar:

Qui sic solvit latentia	Let him who has solved the secret
Ornetur veste regia.	Be adorned with regal robes.

Daniel returns to his quarters. The king orders the stolen Jewish vessels removed from his court and brought to Daniel.

Suddenly, King Darius appears in Belshazzar's court. Before Darius enters, his princes and musicians march in, singing Darius' praises.

Ecce Rex Darius	Behold King Darius
Venit cum principibus,	Approaching with his princes,
Nobilis nobilibus.	The noble with his nobles.
Ejus et curia	And his entire court
Resonat laetitia,	Resounds with joyousness,
Adsunt et tripudia.	And dances are there too.
Hic est mirandus,	He is admired,
Cunctis venerandus.	Venerated by all.
Illi imperia	There are many kingdoms
Sunt tributaria.	Subject to him.
Regem honorant	All honor the King
Omnes et adorant.	And adore him.
Illum Babylonia	Him Babylon fears
Metuit et patria.	And his fatherland.
Simul omnes gratulemur;	Let us all give thanks together;
Resonent et tympana;	Let the drums sound forth;
Citharistae tangant cordas;	Let the harp players pluck their strings;
Musicorum organa	Let the instruments of the musicians
Resonent ad ejus praeconia.	Resound in his praise.

79

Daniel's prophecy is fulfilled with the capture of Belshazzar by King Darius. The court informs the new king of Daniel's powers. The king calls for Daniel and appoints him as his counselor.

Daniel's good fortune has aroused the jealousy of others in the court. They claim that Daniel has defied the king's decree that no other gods should be worshipped save the king himself. Darius attempts to defend Daniel, but the envious counselors prevail.

Darius: Nunquam vobis concedatur   It will never be granted to you
          Quod vir sanctus sic perdatur.   That this holy man should perish so.

Counselors: Lex Parthorum et Medorum   The law of the Parths and the Medes
               jubet in annalibus   in the annals does command
          Ut qui sprevit quae decrevit   He who heeds not the King's decree
               Rex, detur leonibus.   to the lions should be thrown.

Darius: Si sprevit legem quam   If he disdained the law proclaimed
               statueram   Let him be punished as ordained.
          Det poenas ipse quas decreveram.

As Daniel is thrown in the lion's den, he calls out:

Daniel: Hujus rei non sum reus;   For this charge I am not guilty;
          Miserere mei Deus;   Have mercy on me, O God;
               eleyson.   eleison.
          Mitte, Deus, huc patronum   Send, O God, a protector here
          Qui refrenet vim leonum;   To restrain the lions' power;
               eleyson.   eleison.

An angel appears and shields Daniel from the lions.

Another angel brings Habakkuk the prophet to Daniel, bearing food.

Habakkuk: Surge, frater, ut cibum capias;   Rise up, brother, and take the food;
          Tuas Deus vidit angustias;   God has seen your afflictions;
          Deus misit, da Deo gratias,   God has sent it, give thanks to God,
               Qui te fecit.   The God who made you.

In sadness, the king comes to the lion's den to ask Daniel if he thinks his God will save him. Daniel replies:

Daniel:

Rex, in eternum vive!

Angelicum solita misit
  pietate patronum,
Quo Deus ad tempus conpescuit
  ora leonum.

Long live the King!

An angelic protector He has sent
  in His customary mercy
By whom God constrained in time
  the mouths of the lions.

Darius:

Danielem educite,
Et emulos immittite.

Bring Daniel out,
Throw the envious in.

Counselors:

Merito haec patimur, quia
  peccavimus in sanctum Dei,
Injuste egimus,
  iniquitatem fecimus.

We suffer justly for we have sinned
  against this holy man of God,
We have acted wickedly,
  we have done iniquity.

Darius:

Deum Danielis qui regnat in
  saeculis
Adorari jubeo a cunctis populis.

I command that the God of Daniel
Who reigns forever be adored by all.

Prepare your own performance of *The Play of Daniel,* or choose another ancient story and compose a play in a similar style.

Use medieval modes as the basis for your melodies.

Dorian

Mixolydian

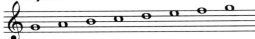

Discuss the characteristics of the music from *The Play of Daniel* and try to incorporate these ideas into your own composition.

Madama Butterfly

Libretto by L. Illica and G. Giacoso
Music by Giacomo Puccini

Giacomo Puccini (1858–1924) was the last major Italian operatic composer in the Romantic tradition. Puccini's best-known operas include *La Boheme, Tosca, Manon Lescaut,* and *Turandot.*

Cast of Characters

Madama Butterfly (Cio-Cio-San), *a young Japanese bride*
Lieutenant B.F. Pinkerton, *an American Naval Officer*
Sharpless, *U.S. Consul At Nagasaki*
Goro, *a marriage broker*
Suzuki, *Butterfly's servant*
Prince Yamadori, *a suitor*
Bonzo, *Butterfly's uncle, a priest*
Imperial Commissioner
Butterfly's child
Friends and relatives
Kate Pinkerton

This opera takes place in Japan in the late 1800s, when Japan had begun to allow foreign ships to enter Japanese ports and engage in trade. American sailors found Japan to be an exotic country, with traditions and customs very different from the ways at home.

This story concerns an American naval officer and his marriage to a young Japanese woman. As you read the drama and listen to excerpts from the opera, think about whether this story could have been set in another country at another time.

Act I

The setting is a house with a terrace and garden on a hill near Nagasaki. The harbor and the city can be seen at the rear of the set. Goro, a marriage broker, is showing the house to U.S. Navy Lieutenant Pinkerton. Goro has arranged a marriage between Pinkerton and a geisha girl, Cio-Cio-San.

Pinkerton: Is everything ready?

Goro: Everything. The registrar and consul are coming, along with your bride-to-be and her relatives. All you have to do is sign the contract and your wedding is over.

Sharpless: *(enters, breathing heavily)* I'm getting too old to climb these rocky hills.

Pinkerton: How do you like my house? I bought it for 999 years, with the option of breaking the contract every month. Then, with Goro's help, I'm to be married in the Japanese manner—also for 999 years; and also, with the option to annul this contract in any month I choose.

Pinkerton: Dovunque al mondo lo Yankee vagabondo si gode e traffica sprezzando rischi. Affonda l'áncora alla ventura . . .

We Yankees roam the world, enjoying ourselves, laughing at risks, taking the profits. We drop anchor wherever we please . . . *(pausing to offer a drink)* . . .

Milk-punch, o Whiskey? Affonda l'áncora alla ventura finché una raffica scompigli nave e ormeggi, alberatura. . . . La vita ei non appaga se non fa suo tesor i fiori d'ogni plaga . . .

Milk-punch or whisky? . . . until it's time to move on. All the treasures and flowers of every shore are ours . . .

Sharpless: È un facile vangelo . . .

That's an easy creed . . .

Pinkerton: . . . d'ogni bella gli amor.

. . . girls wherever we go . . .

Sharpless: È un facile evangelo che fa la vita vaga ma che intristisce il cor . . .

an easy creed for a pleasant life, but it saddens the heart . . .

Pinkerton: Vinto si tuffa, la sorte racciuffa. Il suo talento fa in ogni dove. Cosi mi sposo all'uso giapponese per novecentonovantanove anni. Salvo a prosciogliermi ogni mese.

If unsuccessful, we're up and away, looking for whatever might come along. So, I'm marrying Japanese style, with the right to leave every month.

Sharpless: È un facile vangelo.

An easy creed.

Pinkerton: America for ever!

(toasts with his glass) America forever!

Sharpless: America for ever!

America forever!

Sharpless is concerned about Pinkerton's bride. He doesn't want Pinkerton to take advantage of her. Sharpless toasts Pinkerton's happiness, but Pinkerton adds a toast to the day when he will marry a real American wife. Butterfly appears with her friends and kneels at his feet. She sings of being the happiest maiden in Japan.

Butterfly: Siam giunte. B.F. Pinkerton, Giù. — *(to her friends)* Down.

Friends: Giù. — *(kneeling)* Down!

Butterfly: Gran ventura. — *(to Pinkerton)* Good fortune to you.

Friends: Riverenza. — At your service.

Pinkerton: È un po' dura la scalata? — Was the climb hard?

Butterfly: A una sposa costumata più penosa è l'impazienza. — Nothing is too hard to do for my husband.

Pinkerton: Molto raro complimento. — A nice compliment.

Butterfly: Dei più belli ancor ne so. — I know better ones!

Pinkerton: Dei gioielli! — What a jewel!

Butterfly:	Se vi è caro sul momento . . .	Shall I say another?
Pinkerton:	Grazie, no.	Thank you, no.

Questioned about her family, Butterfly explains that her family used to be rich, but that bad times came upon them. She has worked as a geisha girl to support herself. She tells him that she is fifteen years old. Her mother is living, but her father is dead. While she takes some items she has brought (including a sword) into the house, Goro explains that the sword is the one that was given to her father by the Mikado. As Butterfly returns she sings:

Butterfly:	Ieri son salita tutta sola, in secreto, alla Missione. Colla nuova mia vita posso adottare nuova religione. Lo zio Bonzo nol sa, nè i miei lo sanno. Io seguo il mio destino, e piena d'umiltà, al Dio del signor Pinkerton m'inchino. È mio destino. Nella stessa chiesetta in ginocchio con voi pregherò lo stesso Dio. E per farvi contento potrò forse obliar la gente mia. Amore mio!	Yesterday, I climbed to the Mission. No one knew I went, not even my uncle, the priest. To make you happy, I am giving up my religion and kneeling before your God.
Goro:	Tutti zitti!	Quiet everyone! *(The ceremony begins.)*
Commissioner:	È concesso al nominato Benjamin Franklin Pinkerton, Luogotenente nella cannoniera "Lincoln", marina degli Stati Uniti America del Nord; ed alla damigella Butterfly del quartiere d'Omara, Nagasaki, d'unirsi in matrimonio, per dritto il primo, della propria volontà, ed ella per consenso dei parenti qui testimoni all'atto.	It is granted to Benjamin Franklin Pinkerton, Lieutenant of the gunboat "Lincoln," United States of America, and to Butterfly, living in Omara, Nagasaki, to be joined in marriage. Lieutenant Pinkerton, by his own free will, and Butterfly, with the consent of her relatives, who witness the contract.
Goro:	Lo sposo. Poi la sposa. E tutto è fatto.	*(indicating where to sign)* The husband. Now the wife. And it's all settled.
Friends:	Madama Butterfly!	Madame Butterfly!
Butterfly:	Madama B.F. Pinkerton	Madame B.F. Pinkerton!

Pinkerton proposes a toast to the marriage, to which all respond.

Mother:	O Kami! O Kami!	O Kami! O Kami!
Cousin:	Beviamo ai novissimi legami.	Let us drink to the new union.

The wedding has taken place and the celebration has begun. It is interrupted by the arrival of Butterfly's enraged uncle, Bonzo, a Shinto priest. He curses Butterfly for having left her religion to marry a foreigner.

Priest:	Ciociosan! Ciociosan! Abbominazione!	Cio-Cio-San! You are cursed!
Friends:	Lo zio Bonzo!	It's her uncle, Bonzo!
Goro:	Un corno al guastafeste!	He'll spoil everything!
Priest:	Ciociosan!	Cio-Cio-San!
Goro:	Chi ci leva d'intorno le persone moleste?	How can we get rid of him?
Priest:	Ciociosan! Ciociosan! Che hai tu fatto alla Missione?	Cio-Cio-San! What did you do at the mission?
Cousin:	Rispondi, Ciociosan!	Answer, Cio-Cio-San!
Friends: Pinkerton:	Che mi strilla quel matto?	What is that maniac yelling about?
Priest:	Rispondi, che hai tu fatto?	Answer, what have you done?
Friends: Relatives:	Rispondi, Ciociosan!	Answer, Cio-Cio-San!
Priest:	Come, hai tu gli occhi asciutti? Son dunque questi i frutti? Ci ha rinnegato tutti!	Why aren't you crying? Aren't you ashamed? You have given up everything!
Friends: Relatives:	Hou! Ciociosan!	*Oh! Cio-Cio San!*
Priest:	Rinegato vi dico, il culto antico.	You have given up your religion!
Friends: Relatives:	Hou! Ciociosan!	*Oh! Cio-Cio San!*
Priest:	Kami sarundasico!	You are cursed!

Seeing that Butterfly has become very upset, Pinkerton orders everyone to leave the house. As they leave, the guests repeat angry cries, and Butterfly bursts into tears.

Pinkerton:	Bimba, bimba, non piangere per gracchiar di ranocchi.	Sweetheart, don't cry about the croaking of a few frogs.
Butterfly:	Urlano ancor!	I can still hear them.
Pinkerton:	Tutta la tua tribù e i Bonzi tutti del Giappon non valgono il pianto di quegli occhi cari e belli.	All your family and all the Bonzos in Japan aren't worth a single tear from your dear and beautiful eyes.

Butterfly is consoled by Pinkerton's words, and as night falls the pair
take comfort in being together.

Pinkerton:	Dammi ch'io baci le tue mani care Mia Butterfly! Come t'han ben nomata Tenue farfalla.	Give me your hands and let me kiss them. My Butterfly, how like a slender butterfly you are!
Butterfly:	Dicon ch'oltre mare Se cade in man dell'uom, Ogni farfalla da uno Spillo è trafitta Ed in tavola infitta!	They say that in your country, people catch butterflies and fasten them with pins and set them in display cases.

Pinkerton:	Un po' di vero c'è. E tu lo sai perchè? Perchè non fugga più. Io t'ho ghermita. Ti serro palpitante. Sei mia.	Only to keep them from flying away. I have caught you . . . *(He clasps Butterfly in his arms.)* and you are mine.
Butterfly:	Si, per la vita.	Yes, for my whole life.
Pinkerton:	Vieni, vieni. Via dall'anima in pena L'angoscia paurosa È notte serena! Guarda: dorme ogni cosa!	Come to me and forget all your fears. The night is clear and everything is sleeping.
Butterfly:	Ah! Dolce notte!	Ah, what a lovely night!
Pinkerton:	Vieni, vieni.	Come to me.
Butterfly:	Quante stelle! Non le vidi Mai si belle! Trema, brilla Ogni favilla Col baglior D'una pupilla. Oh!	What stars! I have never seen so many stars shining so beautifully.
Pinkerton:	Via l'angoscia dal tuo cor!	Forget all your fears.
Butterfly:	Quanti occhi Fisi attenti, . . .	The stars are like eyes, looking at us . . .
Pinkerton:	Ti serro palpitante. Sei mia. Ah!	You are mine.
Butterfly:	D'ogni parte A riguardar!	The stars gaze from all sides . . .
Pinkerton:	Vien, vien, sei mia, ah!	Come, you are mine.
Butterfly:	Pei firmamenti, Via pei lidi, Via pel mare.	From heaven, on land, on sea . . .
Pinkerton:	Vieni, guarda: Dorme ogni cosa! etc.	See how everything is sleeping. (etc.)
Butterfly:	Ah! Quanti occhi Fisi, attenti! etc. Ride il ciel! Ah! Dolce notte! Tutto estatico d'amor.	So many stars, gazing like eyes. (etc.) The sweetest, most beautiful night!
Pinkerton:	Ah! Vien! Sei mia!	Come to me! Be mine!

As the newlyweds walk slowly from the garden toward the house, the curtain falls on Act I.

Act II

Three years have passed. Pinkerton has gone to America, but has promised to come back someday. Inside Butterfly's house, Suzuki is praying for Pinkerton's return. Butterfly, on the other hand, is very trusting and sings of the day when she will see her husband again.

Butterfly:

Un bel dì, vedremo
Levarsi un fil di fumo
Sull'estremo confin del mare.
E poi la nave apparè.
Poi la nave bianca
Entra nel porto,
Romba il suo saluto.
Vedi? È venuto!

One lovely day, we'll see smoke rising over the horizon. A white ship will appear and enter the harbor. The guns will thunder a salute: "You see? He has come!"

Io non gli scendo incontro. Io no. Mi metto là sul ciglio del colle e aspetto, e aspetto gran tempo e non mi pesa la lunga attesa.

I won't go down to meet him. I'll stand at the top of the hill and wait a long time.

È uscito dalla folla cittadina un uomo, un picciol punto s'avvia per la collina.

At last, a tiny figure will appear making his way up the hill.

Chi sarà? Chi sarà? E come sarà giunto che dirà? Che dirà? Chiamerà Butterfly dalla lontana. Io, senza dar risposta me ne starò nascosta un po' per celia, e un po' per non morire al primo incontro, ed egli alquanto in pena chiamerà, chiamerà: "Piccina mogliettina olezzo di verbena" i nomi che mi dava al suo venire.

Who is it? And what will he say? He will call "Butterfly" from the distance. I will stay hidden, to tease him, but also so that I don't die of joy. And he will call me again: "My little wife, my little sweet flower"—all the names he used to call me.

Tutto questo avverrà, te lo prometto.

All this will happen; I promise you.

Tienti la tua paura, io con sicura fede l'aspetto.

Keep your fears to yourself. I wait for him with complete faith.

Goro, the marriage broker, brings Yamadori, a wealthy Japanese man who hopes to marry Butterfly. She rejects the idea, saying that she is married to Pinkerton and is bound by the laws of America, not Japan. Sharpless also comes to Butterfly's house with a letter from Pinkerton. Butterfly becomes so excited, that she does not realize that Sharpless is trying to prepare her for bad news. Sharpless angers Butterfly when he suggests that Pinkerton has forgotten her. He urges her to marry Yamadori. Butterfly rushes out and returns with a blond-haired, blue-eyed child. She explains that Pinkerton is unaware of his son because the baby was born after Pinkerton was reassigned to America. She asks Sharpless to write and tell Pinkerton of his son. She is certain that he will return to the two of them.

A cannon shot is heard from the harbor announcing the arrival of a ship. Butterfly and Suzuki rush to decorate the house with flowers in Pinkerton's honor. Butterfly dresses in her wedding gown, puts a scarlet poppy in her hair, and has Suzuki dress the little boy. As the curtain falls, Suzuki and the child have fallen asleep, leaving Butterfly awake, motionless and watching.

Act III

As the curtain rises, the child and Suzuki are still asleep, and Butterfly silently waits for Pinkerton. It is dawn, and the room gradually fills with light.

Suzuki:	Già il sole, Ciociosan!	It is morning, Cio-cio-san!
Butterfly:	Verrà, verrà, vedrai.	He's coming! *(She picks up the child and carries him from the room.)*
Suzuki:	Salite a riposare, affranta siete . . . al suo venire vi chiamerò.	You're so tired; you must rest . . . I'll wake you when he comes.
Butterfly:	Dormi amor mio, dormi sul mio cor. Tu sei con Dio Ed io col mio dolor. A te i rai degli astri d'or, Bimbo mio dormi!	Sleep, little one, sleep. You are with God, while I am with my grief. But on you shine the star's bright rays. Sleep, my darling, sleep.
Suzuki:	Provera Butterfly. Chi sia? Oh!	Poor Butterfly. *(There is a knock at the door and Suzuki slides the panel back.)* Who is it? Oh!

Sharpless:	Stz!	Hush!
Pinkerton:	Zitta! Non la destar.	Quiet! Don't disturb her.
Suzuki:	Era stanca si tanto! Vi stette ad aspettare tutta la notte col bimbo.	She stood watching for you all night with the child.
Pinkerton:	Come sapea?	How did she know?
Suzuki:	Non giunge da tre anni una nave nel porto che da lunge Butterfly non ne scruti il color, la bandiera.	Not a ship has entered the harbor for three years without her knowing.
Sharpless:	Ve lo dissi?	Didn't I tell you?
Suzuki:	La chiamo.	I'll call her.
Pinkerton:	No, non ancor.	No, not yet.
Suzuki:	Lo vedete, ier sera, la stanza volle sparger di fiori.	Last night, she scattered flowers all over for your arrival.
Sharpless:	Ve lo dissi?	Didn't I tell you?
Pinkerton:	Che pena!	This is terrible!
Suzuki:	Chi c'è là fuori nel giardino? Una donna!	Who's in the garden? A woman!
Pinkerton:	Zitta!	Hush!
Suzuki:	Chi è? Chi è?	Who is she? Who is she?

As Pinkerton leaves, his wife Kate and Butterfly enter. After a few moments, Butterfly realizes who Kate is. Kate explains that Pinkerton wants to take the child back to America with them. Butterfly is heartbroken but agrees on the condition that Pinkerton meet her alone in half an hour. Sharpless and Kate exit; Butterfly tells the weeping Suzuki to go and keep the child company. Butterfly kneels before the statue of Buddha. She then goes and takes down her father's sword, kisses the blade ceremoniously, and reads the inscription on the sword:

Butterfly:	"Con onor muore chi non puo serbar vita con onore."	"To die with honor when one can no longer live with honor."

She raises the sword to her throat. The door opens, and Suzuki pushes the child inside. He runs toward his mother. Butterfly throws down the sword and flings her arms around him.

Butterfly: Tu? Tu?

Piccolo Iddio! Amore mio, fior di giglio e di rosa.

Non saperlo mai per te, pei tuoi puri occhi, muor Butterfly, perchè tu possa andar di là dal mare senza che ti rimorda ai di maturi, il materno abbandono. O a me, sceso dal trono dell'alto Paradiso, guarda ben fiso, fiso di tua madre la faccia! Che te'n resti una traccia, guarda ben! Amore, addio! Addio, piccolo amor! Va. Gioca, gioca.

You? You?

My little idol! I love you, my beloved flower.

This terrible scene is not for your innocent eyes. You must go far away across the sea without a mother's death to haunt you as you grow.

But look carefully at your mother's face now, so that you will have a faint memory of it. I love you. Farewell, my little love. Farewell.

She sets the child on a rug, gives him an American flag to play with, and blindfolds him. Taking her father's sword, she goes behind the screen. The sound of the sword is heard falling and Butterfly staggers out from behind the screen toward her son. She kisses him before she collapses by his side. Pinkerton's voice is heard from outside: Butterfly! Butterfly! Butterfly! The door flies open and Pinkerton and Sharpless burst in. They run towards Butterfly who points weakly to the child and dies. Pinkerton drops to his knees, in despair. Sharpless takes the child into his arms and kisses him as the curtain falls.

The Tender Land

Libretto by Horace Everett

Music by Aaron Copland

Aaron Copland (1900–) was born in Brooklyn, New York. He studied in Paris with Nadia Boulanger, who taught some of the most famous composers of the twentieth century. His best-known works include the ballets *Appalachian Spring* and *Rodeo* and the film score for *The Red Pony*.

The action takes place on a farm in the Midwest. The time is the early 1930s; the month is June, the time of Laurie's graduation and the spring harvest.

Cast of Characters

Laurie Moss, *a high school senior*

Ma Moss, *Laurie's mother*

Beth Moss, *Laurie's little sister*

Grandpa Moss, *Laurie's grandfather*

Martin and Top, *two drifters looking for work*

Mr. and Mrs. Jenks, *the Moss's neighbors*

Act I

The isolated world of this rural family revolves around the graduation of Laurie, but she is unsure of her place in the world. It is late afternoon of the day before her high school graduation. (*Laurie strolls home from school. Ma Moss and Beth are on the porch.*)

Laurie: Once I thought I'd never grow tall as this fence. Time dragged heavy and slow. But April came, and August went before I knew just what they meant, and little by little I grew. And as I grew, I came to know how fast the time could go.

Now the time has grown so short; the world has grown so wide. I'll be graduated soon. Why am I strange inside? What makes me think I'd like to try to go down all those roads beyond that line above the earth and 'neath the sky? Tomorrow when I sit upon the graduation platform stand, I know my hand will shake when I reach out to take that paper with the ribboned band.

Now that all the learning's done, oh, who knows what will now begin? It's so strange, I'm strange inside. The time has grown so short, the world so wide.

(Ma Moss and Beth go into the house. Laurie starts to follow, but hides when she hears two strangers approaching.)

Top and Martin are two hungry drifters who have come to the farm looking for work in the harvest. They see Laurie behind the porch and humorously tease her, trying to wrangle an introduction. Not many strangers come to the farm, so Laurie is timid and skeptical. She asks where they are from.

Top:
Martin: We've been north, we've been south. We're goin' east, we're goin' west. We've been here, we're goin' there. That's where we've been and that's where we're goin'.

Martin and Top are explaining to Laurie that they are looking for work when Grandpa returns. The young men ask for a job in the spring harvest. Grandpa is a bit suspicious about hiring strangers and says, "They bring no good, somehow."

Grandpa: When you put it like that I'll have to admit you're
right for the work, and besides bein' fit you're not such
a stranger, not such a stranger, not such a stranger
anymore . . .

Act II

Family and guests are seated around a large table loaded with food. Ma Moss tries to encourage everyone to have a second helping.

Top: Not for me, Missus Moss, I've already had three helpin's.

Mrs. Jenks: Did you see him put that food away? He must have hid it somewhere.

Top: Where I hid it . . . you'll never find it.

Mrs. Jenks: How many boardin' houses have gone bankrupt 'cause of you two?

Top: Let's see: one, two, three, four . . .

Martin: Five boardin' houses and two jails!

All: Tall tales, tall tales, five boardin' houses and two jails!

Grandpa: Try makin' peace with some of my wine—finest wine anywhere, berry wine.

Mr. Jenks: Let's drink to a good spring harvest!

Grandpa: The first of our family that's ever graduated, and *that's* what I'm drinkin' to tonight, Mr. Jenks!

Mr. Jenks: To Laurie then!

All: Laurie, Laurie . . . Laurie Moss!

Laurie: (*seated quietly behind the table, now steps forward, revealing her new dress*) Thank you, thank you all.

(The group prepares for a dance. Top pulls Martin aside.)

Top: Remember what I told you. You have a dance while I start with the old man, then you take him over. (*looking at Laurie*) Gee, she's a pretty thing.

Martin: Take it easy, Top, don't lose us our jobs. (*to himself*) She *is* a pretty thing.

The festive atmosphere continues with a square dance.

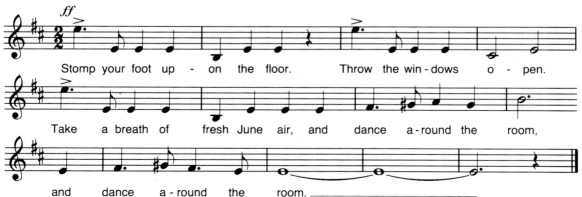

Stomp your foot up - on the floor. Throw the win - dows o - pen.

Take a breath of fresh June air, and dance a - round the room,

and dance a - round the room.

After the dance, all gather around Top, who seems to be telling another story. Martin and Laurie walk away from the group.

Martin: The world seems still tonight. (*He takes Laurie's hand and they go to the porch. At the bottom of the steps he kisses her tenderly.*)

Laurie: Oh, Martin. I should say something.

Martin: Quiet, quiet . . . tomorrow you'll be graduated and like you ma says, "you won't be nervous anymore."

98

Martin begins to dream wistfully and tells Laurie that someday he would like to have a wife who would walk out on the land with him at the end of each day.

Martin: Oh, Laurie, are you ready for settlin' in with me? Do you feel in love that way I do?

Laurie: In love? In love? Yes, yes, I do love you. You came and made me feel in love. I feel so many, many, things, Martin. Tomorrow after graduation . . . perhaps I'll know.

Martin: Laurie, Laurie! I'll be goin' soon.

Laurie: Don't talk of that, Martin. Oh please, I don't want you to go. Harvest is through so quickly.

Martin: I'll stop here 'till harvest's done. If you love me, then this is where I'll stay.

Laurie: Martin, yes, I want you . . . I need you.

Martin: I love you . . . I'll stay.

Laurie: I love you . . .

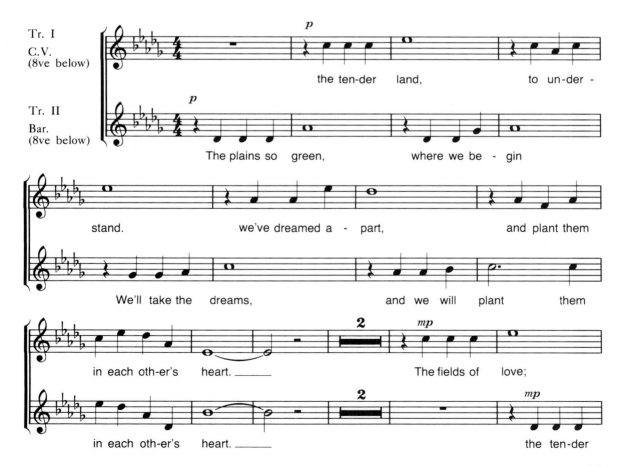

Grandpa discovers that Laurie and Martin are not with the group. He jumps to false conclusions and calls the two drifters "dirty strangers" and "bums." Laurie tries to defend Martin. The party ends abruptly because of the argument. Grandpa orders Martin and Top to leave at daybreak. Laurie turns and runs into the house. Later, Martin and Laurie meet. Laurie convinces Martin to take her with him in the morning. Laurie goes into the house, and Martin is left alone.

Martin: Daybreak will come in such short time. Why do I hope the hours pass slow? Oh, will I find that when I stayed, I meant to go? (*Top enters, having overheard Martin.*) Laurie, I love you, I love you.

Top: What you doin' sittin' here? Don't you want to get some sleep before we hit the road?

Martin: (*dazed, not looking at Top*) Laurie . . . Laurie . . .

Top: What's the matter with you? What's this about Laurie?

Martin: (*still not looking at Top*) She's comin' with us, Top.

Top: Are you crazy? She can't come with us! That Grandpa of hers would have us in jail 'fore we was a mile off! Think, Martin, think . . . our kind's no good for a girl like her. She don't fit with guys like us. She belongs in a soft, white dress up on that graduation stand, with a mother and a grandpa to make a fuss, when she gets that roll with a ribbon band. And look at you . . . you're crazy! Talkin' so big. Big when you talk, walkin' down an endless road. Do what you must, just what you do. Don't take on an extra load. What have you got? What can you give? What will you eat? Where will you live? Is that how you see Laurie? C'mon, hurry boy–day's a comin'. C'mon, we've got no time . . . Take it from me, kid, and try to forget. Try to forget. Hurry! It'll soon be day.

Martin: Laurie, Laurie, forgive me . . . forgive me . . .

(*Top picks up their bundles and they both leave.*)

Daylight is coming as Laurie excitedly descends the steps carrying a small satchel. *(She goes to the shed and knocks lightly.)*

Laurie: Martin, it's daybreak. Are you ready? *(She knocks louder.)* Martin? Martin! Martin! *(Suddenly she throws the door open and falls down weeping. Beth, running out of the house, rushes to her.)*

Beth: Laurie, Laurie, Sister! Oh Laurie, what's wrong? What have I done? Mother!

Laurie: Sh, Beth! Can it end this way? No, I must leave now!

Beth: Oh, Sister, what is wrong? Have you forgotten what day this is?

Laurie: *(to herself)* I must leave now.

Beth: *(pulling away)* You scare me, Laurie.

Ma Moss: *(coming down the steps)* Laurie, Beth, what has happened?

Beth: *(rushing to her mother)* They've gone, they've gone, and Laurie says she's going too!

Ma Moss: What? Is it true they've left? Is this our Laurie?

Laurie: *(calmly)* Yes, Mother, they have left, and I must also leave.

Ma Moss: What are you saying, Laurie? It's graduation day!

Laurie: *(firmly)* I mean it, Mother; I am leaving, too.

Ma Moss: All the things we've planned . . . What do you mean? You promised me . . . Believe I understand. You may think you loved that boy, but Laurie . . .

Laurie: I know, Mother, but try to see . . . how changed this day must seem for me. How changed I, too, have come to be. Goodbye, Beth. Sister, goodbye.

Ma Moss: You are strange to me. I cannot understand. I cannot even recognize your face.

Laurie: Goodbye, Mother, and please ask Grandpa to forgive me that I go.

Ma Moss: I can ask no question, I can hear no answer.

Laurie: Goodbye to all the other things that I have loved. *(She exits slowly.)*

Ma Moss thinks sadly of all the plans that were laid and all the dreams that were made for graduation day. ("What love we put into each thought, each plan . . . ") Her regret takes a more hopeful turn when she thinks, "This love and care we put into each thought, each plan, each making . . . is just beginning . . . "

Is just be - gin - ning, be - gin - ning. _____

As Laurie goes to find her own life, Ma Moss turns to her younger daughter, knowing that although one responsibility has ended, another has begun.

Use Your Listening Skills In the Audience

The audience is an essential element of any musical performance. A good audience must have . . .

Attending Skills

- Arrive at the concert hall or theater in time to be seated and read the program notes before the curtain rises.
- Be considerate of others: talk only during the times for applause and intermissions.

Listening Skills

- Listen for important **themes**. Notice how they are repeated, altered, and varied.
- Listen for music of various historical periods. Is the music all the same, or do you hear music of different times and places?

Responding Skills

Show your appreciation by applauding

- when the conductor reaches the podium
- when the soloists walk on stage
- at the end of a scene, at the theater
- at the end of a composition, at a concert

The Chickawa Symphony Orchestra
Harvey Higgenbottom, Music Director
and Principal Conductor

Overture to *Les Indes Galantes* . . . . Jean Philippe Rameau
(1683-1764)

Rondo from the *Concerto for Horn in E♭* Major . . . . Wolfgang Amadeus Mozart
(1756-1791)

Jane Doe, soloist

Prelude to Act III of *Lohengrin* . . . . Richard Wagner
(1813-1883)

Intermission

Symphony in D major, ... Sergei Prokofiev
Op.25 ("Classical") (1891-1953)

Allegro
Larghetto
Gavotte (Allegro non troppo)
Finale (Molto vivace)

"Tonight's the night! The most famous symphony orchestra in the county is in our town. I'm going to be in the audience . . . What should I wear? How will I know where to sit . . . what to do . . . Wonder if I'll have to be absolutely quiet the whole evening . . . What if I clap at the wrong time . . . will people laugh at me? get mad? How will I know what to listen for?"

Hmmm—I wonder if I look at the program, will that help me know what to do? Just four pieces; gosh, program shouldn't be too long . . . uh-oh, wonder what those extra lines of words under the "Class-i-cal Sym-pho-ny" mean???

What's on the back? "Program notes." Well, maybe that will be a little help. . . . might as well read them. . . . .

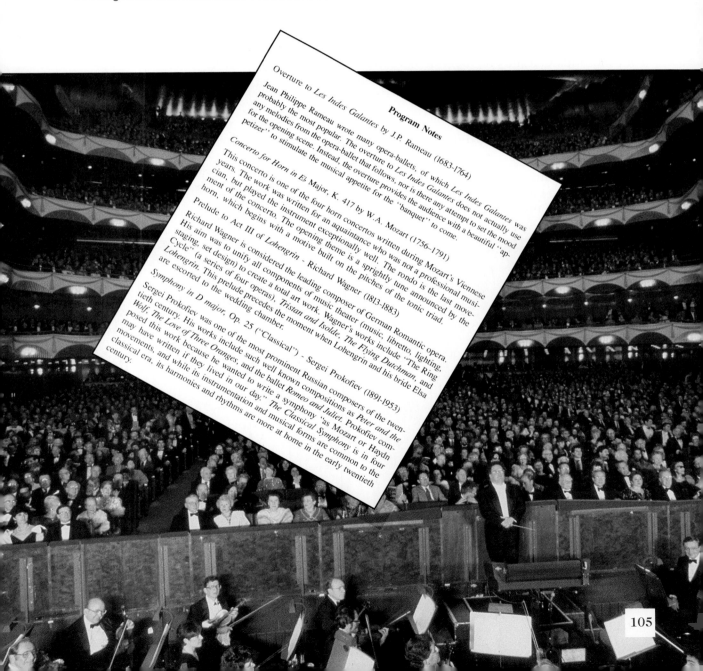

Program Notes

Overture to *Les Indes Galantes* by J.P. Rameau (1683-1764)

Jean Philippe Rameau wrote many opera-ballets, of which *Les Indes Galantes* was probably the most popular. The overture to *Les Indes Galantes* does not actually use any melodies from the opera-ballet that follows, nor is there any attempt to set the mood for the opening scene. Instead, the overture provides the audience with a beautiful "appetizer," to stimulate the musical appetite for the "banquet" to come.

Concerto for Horn in E♭ Major, K. 417 by W.A. Mozart (1756-1791)

This concerto is one of the four horn concertos written during Mozart's Viennese years. The work was written for an aquaintance who was not a professional musician, but played the instrument exceptionally well. The rondo is the last movement of the concerto. The opening theme is a sprightly tune announced by the horn, which begins with a motive built on the pitches of the tonic triad.

Prelude to Act III of *Lohengrin* - Richard Wagner

Richard Wagner is considered the leading composer of German Romantic opera. His aim was to unify all components of music theater (music; libretto, lighting, staging, set design) to create a total art work. Wagner's works include "The Ring Cycle" (a series of four operas), *Tristan and Isolde*, *The Flying Dutchman*, and *Lohengrin*. This prelude precedes the moment when Lohengrin and his bride Elsa are escorted to the wedding chamber.

Symphony in D major, Op. 25 ("Classical") - Sergei Prokofiev (1891-1953)

Sergei Prokofiev was one of the most prominent Russian composers of the twentieth century. His works include such well known compositions as *Peter and the Wolf, The Love of Three Oranges*, and the ballet *Romeo and Juliet*. Prokofiev composed this work because he wanted to write a symphony "as Mozart or Haydn may have written if they lived in our day." *The Classical Symphony* is in four movements, and while its instrumentation and musical forms are common to the classical era, its harmonies and rhythms are more at home in the early twentieth century.

Clues to Musical Style—Putting It All Together

In this unit you have learned that there are many clues to musical style. Clues may be heard in

- the choices of timbre
- the way rhythm and melody are organized
- the kind of texture selected

Listen to compositions that you have not heard before. Which of these clues will help you to identify the origin of each work? You may find that in some music the choice of instruments is the most helpful clue. For other music, it may be the kind of texture used. As you listen, look again at your "Musical Clue" charts to help you recall the characteristics of each musical element.

Composers sometimes borrow ideas from the music of earlier times. This is what the composers did for the two pieces you are about to hear. Can you decide

- when the music was composed?
- where the composer may have found his or her ideas?
- which earlier period is suggested by the music?

Portrait of Mlle. Riviere (1805)
by Jean-Auguste-Dominique Ingres

I Like Ingres, a copy (1962)
by Larry Rivers

Unit 3

The Musician Performs and Creates

The Musician Sings

Most people participate in some form of musical performance throughout their lives.

Some individuals may choose performance as a career. They perform as professional musicians, earning their living as performers, conductors, or teachers.

Others may become amateur performers. They enjoy playing in community bands, choirs, and orchestras, or perhaps just "jamming" with friends.

Still others find performance a satisfying form of recreation. Perhaps they strum the guitar while sitting in the park, pick out a tune on the electric organ, or "whistle while they work"!

The purpose of this unit is to provide you with some of the musical skills that will allow you to continue to perform music in a variety of ways throughout your life.

Begin by finding your best singing range. Experiment by singing "America" in three different keys. Which is your most comfortable singing range? Use the following beginning pitches.

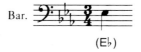

Peace on Earth

Words by Lee Hays

Music by Hans Eisler

D **A7** **D** **(F♯m)**

Peace on earth for - ev - er Is the

peace on earth for - ev - er, When __ the ____

broth - er - hood of

rule when all who ____

D7 **C7** **A7** *go to line 2*

hope of all man - kind. There'll be

go to line 3

peo - ple are of sin - gle mind. The

go to line 4

man up - on the earth, Shall

go back to line 1

long for peace to - geth - er build ____

Rufus Rustus and Chicken

How are these two parts alike? How are they different?

Tr. I
Bar.
(8ve lower)

Ru - fus Rus - tus   John - son   Brown, oh,

Tr. II
C.V.

"C,"   that's the way   it be - gins, and

what you gon - na do when the rain comes   down?

"H,"   that's the next   let - ter in, _____

What you gon - na do   and   what you gon - na say if you

"I,"   you're in   the mid - dle of the word, and

can't pay the rent 'til the rain goes a - way? Oh,

"C,"   you've   al - read - y heard, and

When You and I Were Young Maggie Blues

Words by Jack Frost

Music by Timmy McHugh

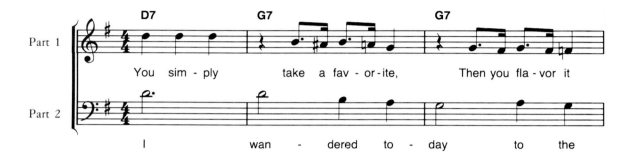

You sim-ply take a fav-or-ite, Then you fla-vor it

I wan-dered to-day to the

with just a note or two of blue har-mo-ny, __ Tell the or-ches-tra to

hill, Mag - gie, to watch the

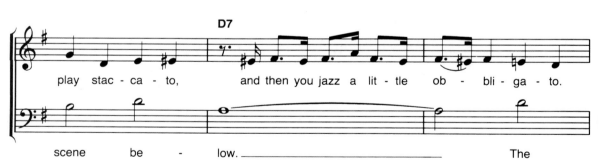

play stac-ca-to, and then you jazz a lit-tle ob-bli-ga-to.

scene be - low. _____ The

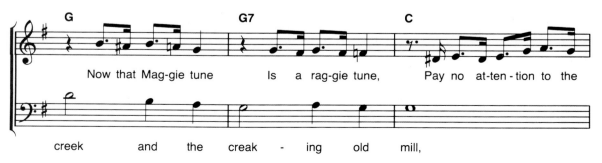

Now that Mag-gie tune Is a rag-gie tune, Pay no at-ten-tion to the

creek and the creak - ing old mill,

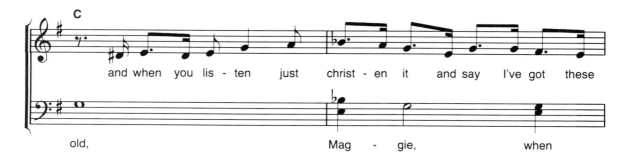

and when you lis - ten just christ - en it and say I've got these

old, Mag - gie, when

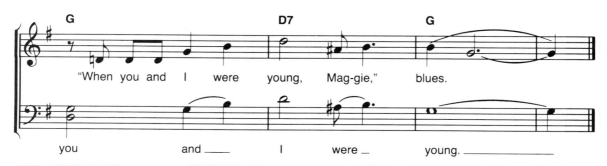

"When you and I were young, Mag-gie," blues.

you and ___ I were ___ young. ___

Looky, Looky Yonder

American Folk Song

Which part of this song is in your vocal range?

Select a part to perform as everyone sings the song.

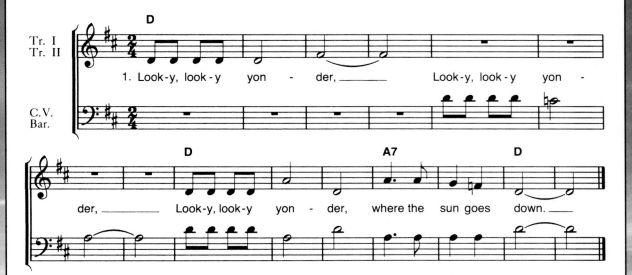

Tr. I
Tr. II

1. Look-y, look-y yon - der, _____ Look-y, look-y yon -

C.V.
Bar.

der, _____ Look-y, look-y yon - der, where the sun goes down. _____

2. Ax is a-walkin', *(3 times)*
   Where the sun goes down.

3. Chips are a-talkin', *(3 times)*
   When the sun goes down.

4. Hear us singing, *(3 times)*
   When the sun goes down.

5. In the evening, *(3 times)*
   When the sun goes down.

The Water Is Wide

American Folk Song

2. I once leaned against a young oak tree,
    It seemed as strong as my love seemed,
    It bended and then it broke, you see,
    My love was not the dream I dreamed.

3. The water is wide, I cannot get over,
    There's no true love, at least not for me,
    My love was untrue but I can't complain,
    Some day I hope to love again.

Hand Me Down My Walkin' Cane

Southern Mountain Song

2. Oh, if I die in Tennessee, *(3 times)*
   Just ship me back, C.O.D.
   All my sins been taken away,
      taken away.

Rock Around the Clock

Words and Music by Max Freedman and Jimmy De Knight

One, two, three o'-clock, four o'-clock, rock, Five, six, sev-en o'-clock,

eight o'-clock, rock. Nine, ten, e-lev-en o'-clock, twelve o'-clock, rock,

We're gon-na rock a-round the clock to-night.— 1. Put — your

glad rags on and join me, hon', — We'll have some fun when the
clock strikes two and three and four, — If the band slows down we'll —

clock strikes one. } We're gon-na rock a-round the
ask for more, }

clock to-night, — We're gon-na rock, rock, rock till

broad day-light, — We're gon-na rock, gon-na rock a-round —

— the clock— to-night. — 2. When — the —

Improvise a three-part harmonic accompaniment to go with this rock tune from the Fifties. Divide into three groups to sing the changes in pitch. You may wish to hum, sing words on the harmony pitches, or create your own ideas.

One, two, three o'-clock, four o'-clock, rock,

Five, six, sev-en o'-clock, eight o'-clock, rock.

Nine, ten, e-lev-en o'-clock, twelve o'-clock, rock,

We're gon-na rock a-round the clock to-night.

Put your glad rags on and join me, hon',
We'll have some fun when the clock strikes one.

We're gon-na rock a-round the clock to-night,

We're gon-na rock, rock, rock till broad day-light,

We're gon-na rock, gon-na rock a-round_____ the clock to - night.

Mango Walk

Traditional

tell me,   do tell, Do   tell me,   Do tell that   you   don't   go   to

Tell   for true,   tell   for true,   you   don't   go   to

no mang - . . .   No, Sir, and   steal all   num - ber   'lev - en.

no,   go walk   steal   the num - ber   'lev - en.

LISTENING

Jamaican Rumba

by Arthur Benjamin

"Jamaican Rumba" is based on musical ideas found in "Mango Walk." Two main melodies are heard in the piece.

Melody A

Melody B

Which of these melodies is like the upper part of "Mango Walk"? Which one is similar to the lower part?

These two melodies are heard both alone and together as partners in "Jamaican Rumba." Can you determine which melody each of these instruments is playing?

Canon in D

by Johann Pachelbel

Johann Pachelbel (1653–1706) was a German composer of the Baroque era. Although he was primarily an organist, Pachelbel composed many works for chorus and instrumental ensembles.

Listen to this composition. It is based on a series of melodic ideas, each of which is eight beats long. All of the ideas are based on the same chord sequence.

The **ground bass** shown below is repeated many times. Sing along with it using the syllable "doo" or "loo" until you are very sure of the chord sequence. Try each new melodic idea as it is introduced.

After you have heard all the melodic ideas, close your eyes and improvise a melody that "feels right" to you.

Bells and Pachelbels

by Buryl Red

Listen to the recording. How is this piece different from Pachelbel's
Canon in D? Listen again and improvise your own melodic ideas.

Introduction Measures 1-8

The introduction begins with a sustained chime sound on D, continues with an **ostinato** of steady sixteenth notes, and closes with a single statement of the main theme (Pachelbel's ground bass) in eighth notes.

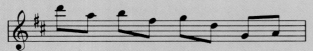

Section A (synthesized sounds) Measures 9-32

The main theme is repeated three times as part of the chord sequence from the *Canon in D.* These chords move in whole notes using bell sounds; a background ostinato moves in steady sixteenth notes.

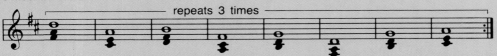

Section B (acoustic sounds) Measures 33-48

The background ostinato now moves in steady sixteenth note triplets. The main theme is heard in half notes using piano and harp sounds. In the last measures of this section, the entrance of bell sounds creates a brief canon.

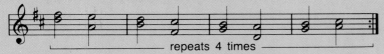

Transition (synthesized and acoustic sounds) Measures 49-51

The main theme and chord sequence from Section A are heard using synthesized vocal sounds moving in quarter notes. (The chord sequence is stated here in two different keys at the same time!) A fanfare of trumpet sounds moving in eighth notes quickly follows, leading us into the coda.

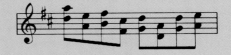

Coda Measures 52-60

The trumpet fanfare from the transition is transformed into a sixteenth note ostinato. This ostinato consists of the main theme played forward and then backward. (See the example above.) The remaining music is based on an extended D major chord and includes references to all the musical materials heard in the piece.

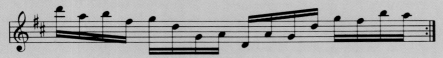

The Musician Performs: Guitar

Learn how to "pick" folk tunes on the guitar.

Playing Position
Hold the guitar comfortably and securely. Rest your left foot on a foot rest or a small coffee can. Place the guitar so that there are four points of contact with the body:
1. Underneath the right forearm
2. Against the chest
3. Inside the right knee
4. On the left knee
If you are holding the guitar correctly, your right hand will fall directly in front of you.

Your body should be vertically aligned, and your shoulders level. Slant the guitar so that the head is slightly higher than your shoulders.

Hand Positions
- Place the thumb on the back of the guitar neck to provide balance and support for fingers pressing down on the strings.
- Press strings with fingertips to avoid touching adjacent strings.
- Fingers on the left hand are numbered in this order:

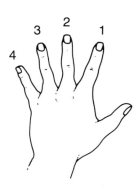

Buffalo Gals

Music by Cool White

Place your right hand just behind the sound hole in a relaxed manner. To play single-line melodies or special bass parts, use the thumb (*p*) and fingers (*i, m, a*) to pluck individual strings.

1. As I was walk-ing down the street, down the street, down the street,
2. I asked her if she'd stop and talk, stop and talk, stop and talk,

A pret-ty gal I chanced to meet, Oh, she was fair to see.
Her feet took up the whole side-walk and left no room for me.

Oh, Buf-fa-lo Gals, won't you come out to-night, come out to-night, come out to-night?

Oh, Buf-fa-lo Gals, won't you come out to-night and dance by the light of the moon?

Use the thumb (*p*) to play an open-string accompaniment to "Buffalo Gals." Repeat the following pattern four times to complete the song.

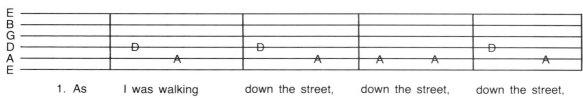

1. As I was walking down the street, down the street, down the street,

Learn to Read Tablature

Tablature is a form of **notation** for guitar that directs the fingers to the correct strings and frets. It does not indicate rhythm. When using tablature, the performer must already know the melody.

When playing from tablature, read the fret numbers in sequence from left to right.

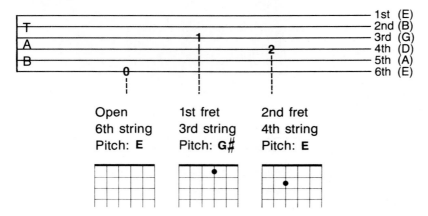

Read the tablature and pluck these pitches with your thumb on the sixth string. Compare the tablature with traditional notation and with finger placement on the fret board of the guitar.

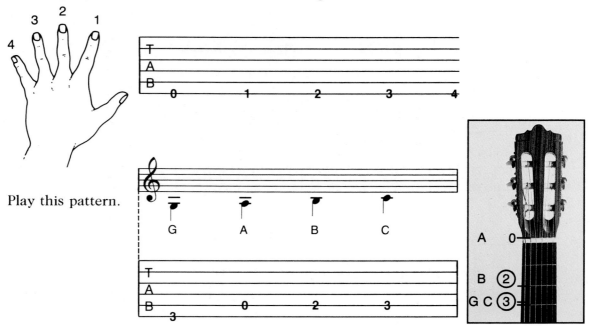

Play this pattern.

126

Down in the Valley

Traditional

Use your thumb to play this walking bass accompaniment.

Read the tablature. Use *i, m, a* to play this melody. Use one finger on each string: D, G, B.

Right Hand

Taps

U.S. Army Bugle Call

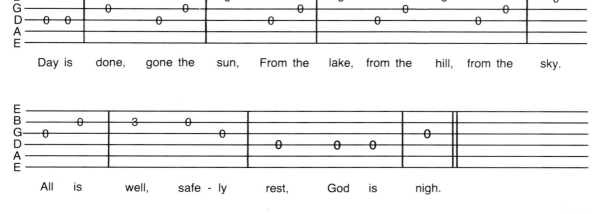

Can the Circle Be Unbroken?

Adapted and Arranged by Dan Fox

Use the rest stroke.

The rest stroke is performed by pulling your finger toward you across one string and coming to rest on the next. Follow the tablature to learn this melody. Use the rest stroke. Alternate fingers *i* and *m* when playing. Make your fingers "walk" on the strings.

128

The Cruel War

Words by Peter Yarrow   Music by Paul Stookey

Practice alternating fingers *i* and *m* as you move among three strings.
Begin on the D string.

Play "The Cruel War."

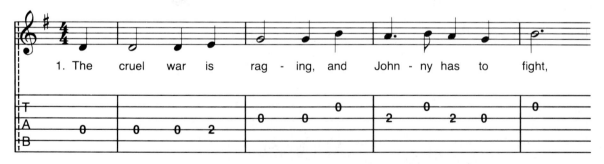

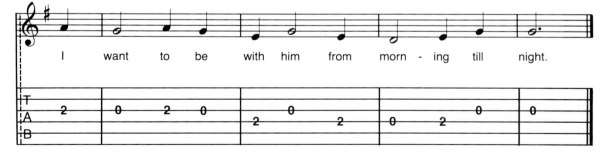

2. I'll go to your captain, get down on my knees,
   Ten thousand gold guineas I'd give for your release.

3. Ten thousand gold guineas, it grieves my heart so;
   Won't you let me go with you? Oh, no, my love, no.

Gotta Travel On

Words and Music by Paul Clayton

I've laid a - round and played a - round this old town too

long, Sum - mer's al - most gone, yes,

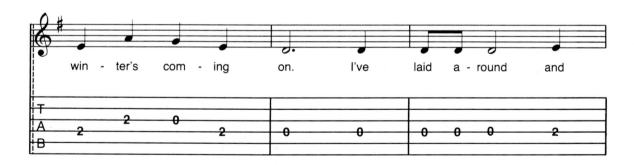

win - ter's com - ing on. I've laid a - round and

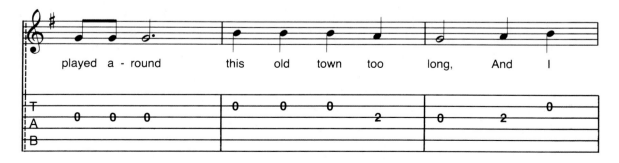

played a - round this old town too long, And I

feel like I've got - ta tra - vel on. _____

LISTENING

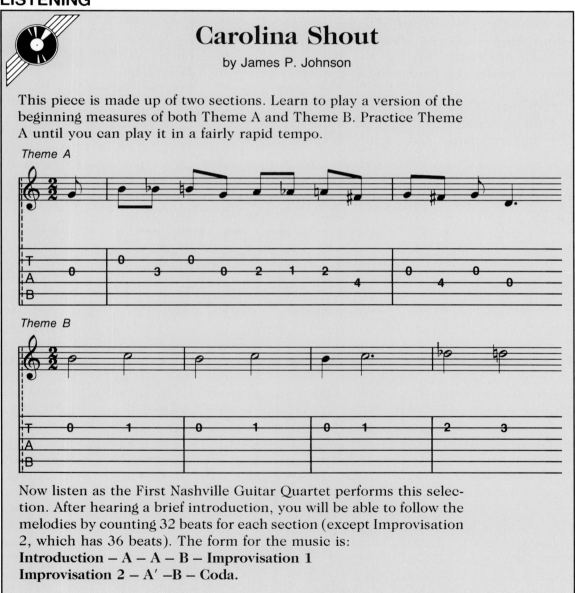

Carolina Shout
by James P. Johnson

This piece is made up of two sections. Learn to play a version of the beginning measures of both Theme A and Theme B. Practice Theme A until you can play it in a fairly rapid tempo.

Theme A

Theme B

Now listen as the First Nashville Guitar Quartet performs this selection. After hearing a brief introduction, you will be able to follow the melodies by counting 32 beats for each section (except Improvisation 2, which has 36 beats). The form for the music is:

Introduction — A — A — B — Improvisation 1
Improvisation 2 — A′ —B — Coda.

The Musician Performs: Percussion

A percussionist plays many different kinds of instruments. Some of these produce sounds that have **definite pitch,** such as tuned drums, gongs, and marimbas. Other instruments, such as rattles, cymbals, and claves, produce sounds of **indefinite pitch.** These instruments have a high, medium, or low range of pitch.

As with other instruments, different sounds can be made on each one. Rattles, such as maracas, can be played so that a dry, single sound is produced. They can also be shaken to create a continuous sound. The sound of percussion instruments can be varied depending on:
- the part of the instrument struck
- the size, shape, and material of the striker
- the force, angle, and duration of these strikes

Be a percussionist. Create and play rhythm patterns.

1 2 3 4 5 6 7 8 | or

1 2 — — 5 6 — — | or

1 — 3 4 — — 7 — | or

1 — — 4 5 — — — | or

1 — — — — — 7 8 | or

Play a rhythm pattern called **clave:**

1 — — 4 — — 7 — | — — 3 — 5 — — — | or

132

Learn to Play Conga Drum

Using the heel of alternate hands, hit the center of the drum and leave your hand on the drumhead. Use the syllable "ta" to describe this sound. (T)

Using the fingertips of alternate hands, hit the center of the drum, and leave fingertips on the drumhead. Use the syllable "ka" to describe this sound. (K)

For a high, cracking sound, use the fingertips of alternate hands to slap the drumhead while the heel of your hand strikes the rim. The syllable "bop" is used to describe this sound. (B)

Using only the fingers of alternate hands, strike the edge of the drumhead and take your fingers off. Use the syllable "de" to describe this sound. (D)

Practice each of the following patterns, then combine and perform them together.

Ex. 1	T K B K T K D D	T K B K T K D D
Ex. 2	1 - - 4 - - 7 -	- - 3 - 5 - - -

Use these patterns to accompany "Comin' Home Baby."

LISTENING

Comin' Home Baby
by Benjamin Tucker and Robert Dorough

Rhythmic Sounds From Ghana

Learn to play the conga drum with master drummer, Mustapha Tetty Addy. Listen to the recording and play along. Add these percussion instruments to create an African percussion ensemble.

Two-tone Bell

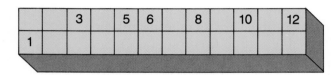

Guiro

Low Conga Drum
right hand
left hand

High Conga Drum

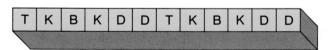

Rattle   palm

        thigh

Meaning of symbols:

T = Ta
K = Ka
D = De
B = Bop

Percussion in an African Style

Read the score.
Use instruments and voices to perform the music.

	1	2	3	4	5	6	7	8	9	10	11	12
Master Drum	1	•	3	4	•	6	7	•	9	10	•	12
Low Drum	1	•	•	4	•	6	7	•	•	10	•	12
Medium-low Drum	1	•	3	•	5	6	7	•	•	10	•	12
Low Drum	1	•	•	4	•	•	7	•	•	10	•	•
Medium Drum	•	2	•	4	•	6	•	8	•	10	•	12
High Drum	1 H	2 L	3 H	4 H	5 L	6 H	7 H	8 L	9 H	10 H	11 L	12 H
Medium-high Drum	•	2	3	•	5	6	•	8	9	•	11	12
Medium-low Drum	1 L	2 L	3 H	4 L	5 L	6 H	7 L	8 L	9 H	10 L	11 L	12 H
Two-toned Bell	1 L	•	3 H	•	5 H	6 H	•	8 H	•	10 H	•	12 H
Large Woodblock	1	•	3	•	5	•	7	•	9	•	11	•
Rattle	1 U	•	3 D	4 U	5 D	6 D	7 U	8 D	9 U	10 D	11 U	12 D
Sing the 5th of a major scale	•	•	•	•	5 Ya	6 ku	•	•	•	•	11 ku	•
Sing the 3rd of a major scale	•	•	•	•	•	•	7 Ke	8 le	9 le	10 Ya	•	•

135

Talking Drums

Hundreds of years before Western cultures developed rapid communication systems, some Africans sent messages from village to village over many miles using talking drums. This was possible because many African languages are tonal.

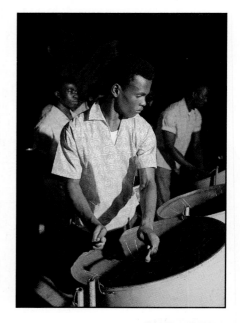

In a tonal language, the meaning of a word depends on the pitch at which each syllable is spoken.

For example, the Lokele people of northern Zaire use the word *lisaka* (lee-sah-kah) to mean three different things:

| Higher sound | | This means "puddle" or |
| Lower sound | li-sa-ka | "marsh." |

| Higher sound | ka | This means "promise." |
| Lower sound | li-sa- | |

| Higher sound | sa-ka | This means "poison." |
| Lower sound | li- | |

You can see how very important it is to speak the higher and lower sounds in the correct place!

Drum language uses these higher and lower sounds to communicate messages. The combination of higher and lower sounds makes it possible to actually communicate messages using talking drums.

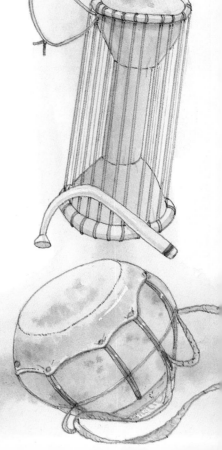

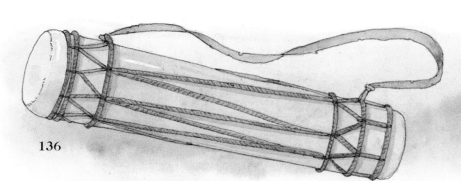

Drum phrases can be very poetic. Drum language often uses vivid word-imagery to make the listener "feel" the message.

For example, in the Lokele language the spoken phrase "don't worry" or "don't be afraid" could be expressed in drum language as "take away the knot of the heart into the air."

Use available drums to produce high and low sounds. Chant and perform the high and low sounds for the word *lisaka* on page 136. Use only steady beats for now.

Create drum **phrases** using spoken words from your own language:

- speak each phrase using natural pitch inflections
- play these phrases on a drum using high and low sounds
- improvise rhythms to enhance your drum phrase

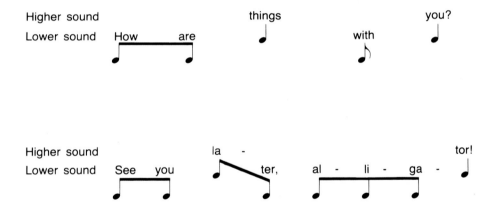

Can you think of other phrases?
Improvise a rhythm for each phrase. Create your own drum language.

Listen to the recorded example of talking drums from Ghana.

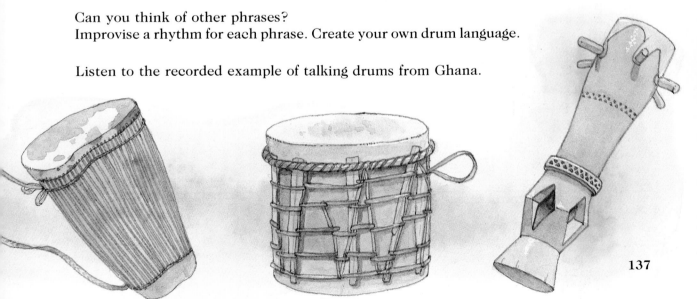

137

The Musician Performs: Dulcimer

Many folk melodies are based on ancient **scales** called **modes**. "The Keys to Canterbury" is based on the **Aeolian** mode.

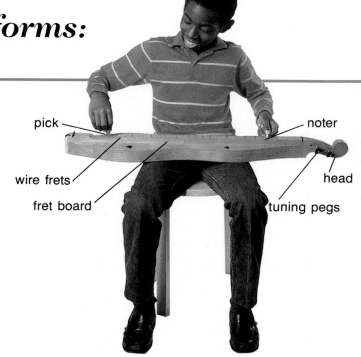

pick — noter

wire frets — head

fret board — tuning pegs

The Keys of Canterbury

English Folk Song

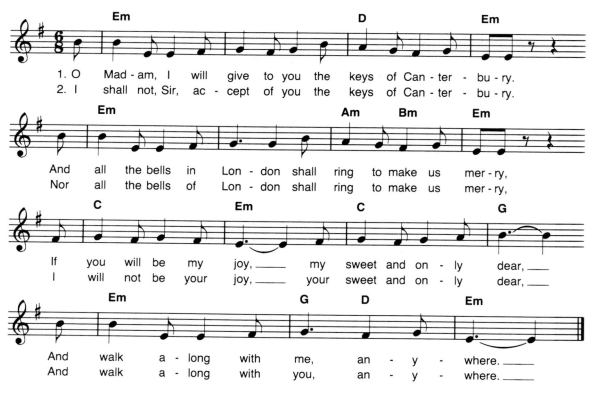

1. O Mad-am, I will give to you the keys of Can-ter-bu-ry.
2. I shall not, Sir, ac-cept of you the keys of Can-ter-bu-ry.

And all the bells in Lon-don shall ring to make us mer-ry,
Nor all the bells of Lon-don shall ring to make us mer-ry,

If you will be my joy, _____ my sweet and on-ly dear, _____
I will not be your joy, _____ your sweet and on-ly dear, _____

And walk a-long with me, an-y-where. _____
And walk a-long with you, an-y-where. _____

Perform a Mode on the Dulcimer

Because the dulcimer is a folk instrument, the songs performed on it are often based on modes. Each mode is made up of five whole steps and two half steps. On the dulcimer, the whole-step frets are larger than the half-step frets.

Whole-step frets look like this:

Half-step frets look like this:

Each mode has a distinctive sound because it has a different arrangement of whole and half steps. Between which tones do the half steps occur in this mode?

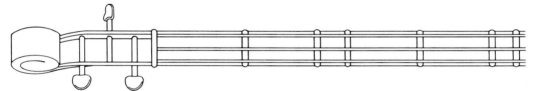

Play this mode on the dulcimer. Hold the dulcimer on your knees with its head to your left. Hold the noter in your left hand so that the thumb is on the top of the stick, pressing down. The noter should touch only the string nearest you. The second knuckle of the index finger should slide along the side of the fret board. To strum, hold the pick in your right hand and move the pick back toward you.

Examine the frets.
On which fret will you begin in order to play the sequence of whole and half steps shown above?
This time, as you move the noter from fret to fret, pluck only the string closest to you.

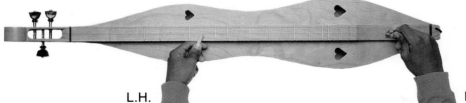

L.H.   R.H. strum

Sound familiar? It should! It's the **Major scale** that you have heard many times. It is also called the **Ionian** mode.

Go Tell Aunt Rhody

Traditional

Read the song tablature and perform a song in the Ionian mode. To play different pitches, slide the noter up and down the string nearest you while strumming all the strings.

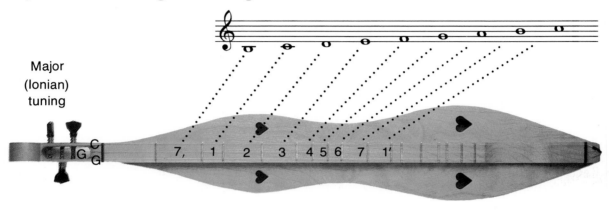

Major (Ionian) tuning

Song Tablature

low   Begin here: high

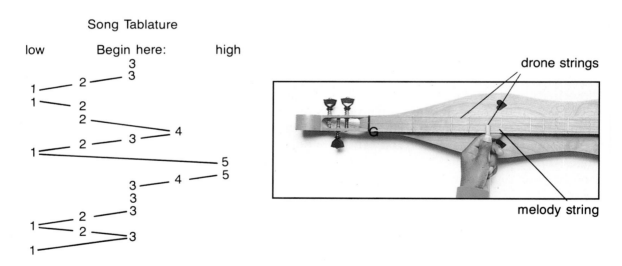

drone strings

melody string

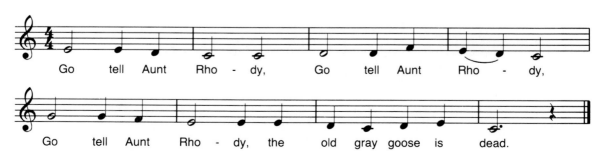

Go tell Aunt Rho - dy, Go tell Aunt Rho - dy,

Go tell Aunt Rho - dy, the old gray goose is dead.

140

Perform in a New Mode

Perform in the **Mixolydian** mode. Where are the half steps in relation to the whole steps in this mode? Can you decide where "1" will be on the dulcimer by studying this arrangement of frets?

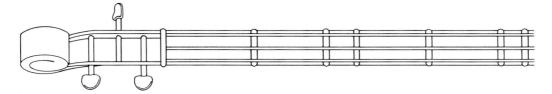

Did you determine that "1" will be played on the open string in this mode?

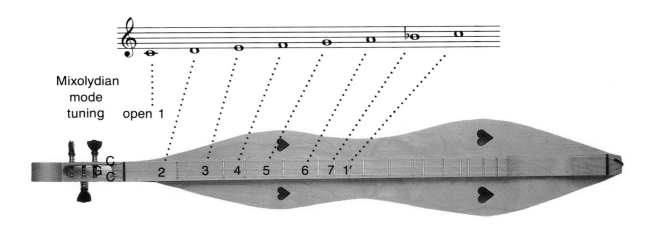

Experiment with the Mixolydian mode.

1. Retune the dulcimer so that the melody will be in tune with the drone strings. Change the pitch of the melody string from G to C.

2. Use the noter and play the pitches of this mode on the melody string. Begin on the open string, playing up and then down.

3. Read the tablature on the following pages. Learn to play "The Highwayman" and "Old Joe Clark," which are folk melodies in the Mixolydian mode.

Perform in the Mixolydian Mode

"The Highwayman" uses all the pitches in the Mixolydian mode. Play the mode. Listen for the unusual sound of the seventh step.

Begin here (open string):

The Highwayman

English Folk Song

1. It's of a jol - ly high - way-man, Like - wise a no - ted rov - er,
2. I rob - bed lords, I rob - bed dukes in a ve - ry rak - ish man - ner,

I drove my par - ents al - most wild, When first I went__ a rov - ing.
Not on - ly to main - tain my - self, Like - wise my a - ged moth - er.

Old Joe Clark

American Folk Song

Compare the melody written in traditional notation with the song tablature shown below.

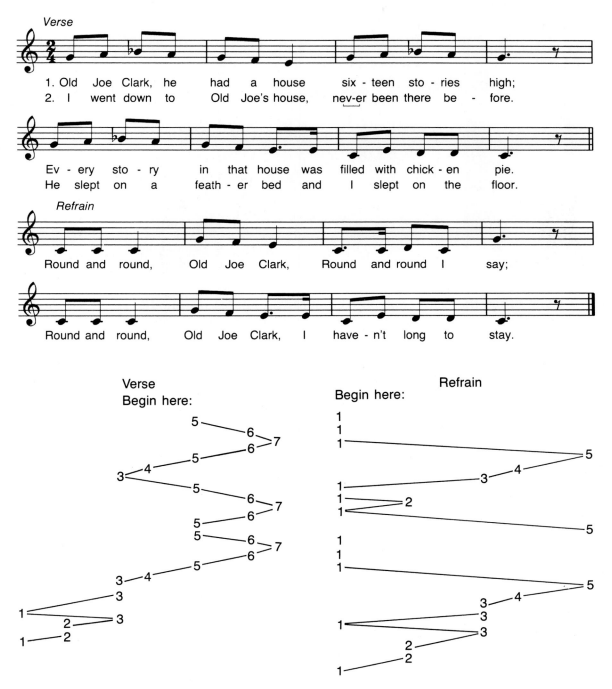

Verse

1. Old Joe Clark, he had a house six - teen sto - ries high;
2. I went down to Old Joe's house, nev-er been there be - fore.

Ev - ery sto - ry in that house was filled with chick - en pie.
He slept on a feath - er bed and I slept on the floor.

Refrain

Round and round, Old Joe Clark, Round and round I say;

Round and round, Old Joe Clark, I have - n't long to stay.

Verse
Begin here:

Refrain
Begin here:

The Musician Composes, Improvises, and Arranges

Milton Babbitt, American composer

For some of us, the word *composer* conjures up images of round-shouldered individuals, peering out through bent spectacles from under shaggy wigs. We forget sometimes that some of our favorite popular performers are composers.

Composing, improvising, and arranging all involve using original musical ideas to create new musical sounds. There are, however, some differences among the three.

Improvising means creating musical ideas "on the spot." You might be whistling your own tune as you walk down the street, "doodling" on the guitar, or making up a vocal or instrumental part as you listen to a recording.

Composing involves planning ahead. The composer may begin with jotting down ideas for a folk song, writing a score for a symphony orchestra, or developing ideas on an electronic **synthesizer**.

Arranging is taking existing music and creating special parts for instruments and voices. The result is a new arrangement, not a new composition.

Look through this chapter. Choose ideas that you find most interesting. Improvise, compose, or arrange your own music for
- voices
- instruments
- computer

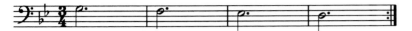
Create an improvisation on this ground bass (repeated bass pattern).
Slowly play this descending pattern on the piano.

Continue to play the ground bass and sing this melody. Create your
own ending.

Li - li - li - li - li - li   (etc. . .)

Repeat this ground bass many times as individuals share their ideas
for completing the melody.

LISTENING

A Ground

by George Frederick Handel

George Frederick Handel
(1685–1759) was a major composer of the Baroque era. Among
his many works is the famous ora-
torio, *The Messiah.*

Listen to "A Ground" by Handel.
How does this compare to the
music you have just sung and
played?

George Frederick Handel

Rap, Rhythm, and Scratch Music

Create a repeated percussion pattern in $\frac{2}{2}$ **meter** to accompany this rap. Select and develop an appropriate "scratch" sound for dancing.

Get your boom box and tie on your dogs,

Here come the dan - cers in their fan - cy togs.

All you break boys, ga - ther round.

'Cause what you see . . . will as - tound.

I'm gon - na va - cil - late my feet to a fun - ky beat,

(Drum improvisation with scratch)

Lest you was - n't watch - in' I will re - peat.

(Drum improvisation with scratch)

Who thinks they're bet - ter? Who gon - na dare?

Look out, Mis - ter Cool, you move like a chair!

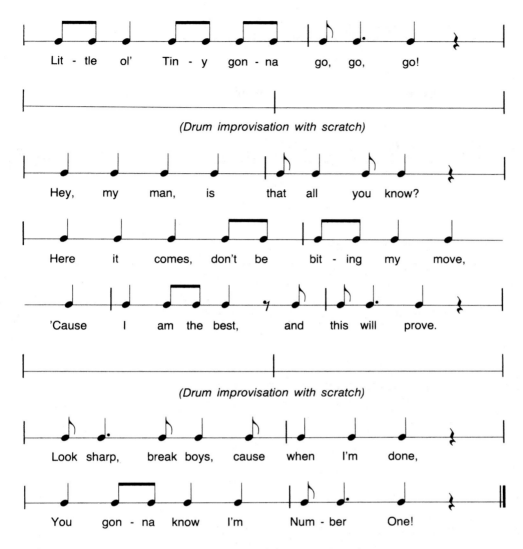

Lit - tle ol' Tin - y gon - na go, go, go!

(Drum improvisation with scratch)

Hey, my man, is that all you know?

Here it comes, don't be bit - ing my move,

'Cause I am the best, and this will prove.

(Drum improvisation with scratch)

Look sharp, break boys, cause when I'm done,

You gon - na know I'm Num - ber One!

Create Your Own Rap, Rhythm, and Scratch Music

Learn to create scratch music. Use an inexpensive record player. Place a piece of cardboard on the turntable. (You may want to use an old recording.) The cardboard allows the turntable to maintain its normal speed at all times, even when the recording is stopped or backspun. Control the record by putting your hand on the record's edge while backspinning.

Carry It On

Words by Marion Wade

Music by Gil Turner

Learn to sing this song.

E

There's a man by my side walk - in'. There's a voice

B7

in - side me talk - in'. There's a word needs a say - in':___

E   B7

Car - ry it on,_____ car - ry it on._____ Car - ry it on,_____

B7   E

car - ry it on._____

CARRY IT ON, Words and Music by Gil Turner
TRO—© Copyright 1964 and 1965 Melody Trails, Inc., New York, NY Used by Permission

Be an Arranger

An arranger of music needs skills in

- reading and writing music
- achieving musical balance among different parts
- combining vocal and instrumental parts in interesting ways

Select one or more class arrangers who have these skills to arrange "Carry It On."

Select soloists to improvise special parts for each phrase:

There's a man (There's a man) by my side . . .

Each soloist must

- listen to the accompaniment
- improvise in relation to the chord sequence
- improvise in relation to the underlying **beat**

Each soloist may

- echo words
- omit words or phrases
- change the rhythm
- stretch one word over several pitches

The arranger should decide

- when the full group will sing
- which soloist will add parts to verses
- whether the ideas of two or more soloists may be combined

Experiment with several ideas; then decide on the arrangement for the whole piece.

The arranger becomes the conductor, providing signals for the group. Perform your completed arrangement.

Be a Lyricist

A lyricist needs skills in communicating by means of

- words that evoke images
- rhyming phrases
- words that create a natural rhythmic flow

A lyricist may write words that are very metrical or words that move in a freely flowing rhythm. Prepare lyrics that will be metrical and result in even phrases. Begin by feeling the length of the phrase.

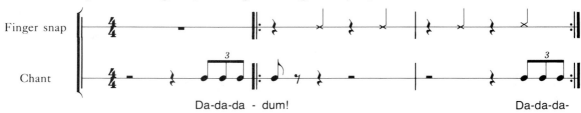

Fill in the empty space with a vocal rhythm such as:

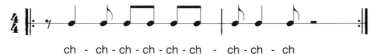

List all the words you can think of that rhyme with "blue." (Sue, glue, true, moo, zoo, too, adieu)

Now begin to change your rhythmic filler (ch's) to a talkin' blues. End your rhythm pattern with one of the rhyming words. Replace the "ch" sounds with words to form a sentence ending with the rhyming word.

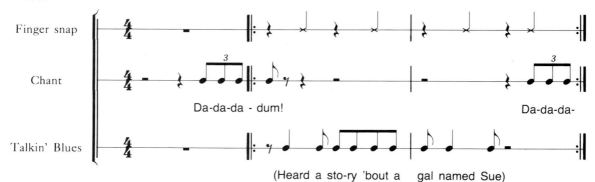

Play a 12-bar blues accompaniment while "talking" six of the blues phrases you have just created.

Create Jazz Riffs

Jazz is a musical idiom that evolved from Afro-American roots. Jazz has its own characteristic style, which is highly improvisational in nature. An important part of jazz technique is the ability to improvise melodic ideas on the pitches within a given **chord** progression.

Liberties are often taken with jazz rhythms. For example, eighth notes are seldom played evenly. Instead of

the performer might play

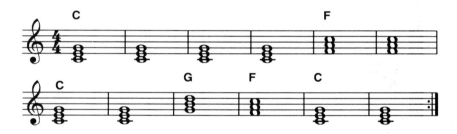

Some jazz melodies are built on repeated patterns called **riffs.** Read and play some riffs based on a blues chord progression. Use jazz syllables (**scat singing**) to establish the rhythm of each riff. Play each riff on either the root, third, or fifth of the chord.

Basic blues in C

Riff on the root

Riff on the third

dop dop du da dop

Riff on the fifth

dop dop du da

Riff on the root and third

dop du da

Compose your own riff. Base your riff on the pitches of each chord in the basic blues in C (shown on page 151).

Blue notes

Jazz melodies sound different to us because some of the notes are "bent," or sung and played lower or higher in pitch. This bending of notes can be as little as a quarter tone or as much as a whole tone. These bent notes are called **blue notes.**

Use blue notes to create jazz riffs. Add a lowered seventh to the harmony. Use this lowered seventh to play a riff on the root.

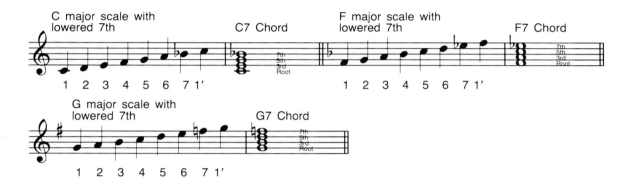

Riff on the root and lowered seventh

du   du da du dop

Compose your own blues riff on the third of each chord. How can you lower the third?

Improvise in Jazz Style

When improvising jazz, a performer often begins with a basic musical structure and then improvises a series of "choruses" using the following techniques:

Melody The original melody might be **ornamented** with added notes.

The shape of the original melody might be preserved, even though some notes are changed.

Structure The original melody might be stretched or compressed, creating phrases of different lengths.

Harmony The chord progression might be made more complex by adding chords or altering some chords.

Rhythm The accents could be changed so that they fall on different beats of the measure.

The rhythmic units could be varied by alternating groups of eighth notes, quarter notes, and triplet figures or by shifting the placement of rests.

Begin by listening to the original theme of "Joan's Blues" while following the notation on page 155. Then listen to the first chorus and compare it to the original theme.

Keep in mind, as you compare the chorus with the original theme, that the chorus was notated after it was performed, by listening to the recording and writing down the musical ideas. The performers improvised the choruses "on the spot."

As you listen to the complete composition, try to decide:

- What is the function of the bass player during the piano solo?
- What is the function of the drummer?
- How does the 16-bar theme become a "12-bar blues"?

Try developing your own improvisation. Begin by composing a four- or eight-measure musical idea. Plan a chord progression; devise a simple melodic shape to use. Then begin to experiment. Use some of the ideas you learned from listening to "Joan's Blues." Work alone or with others.

Joan's Blues
by Joan Wildman

The Computer as a Composing Tool

The computer has become a valuable tool for the composer. It is capable of

- choosing and controlling pitch
- choosing and controlling rhythm
- choosing and controlling harmony
- determining form (sequencing sounds and linking them together)
- choosing and controlling dynamics
- choosing and controlling sound quality (timbre)
- choosing and controlling the attack, decay, and sustain time
- generating musical sounds
- controlling one or more synthesizers
- converting sounds played on keyboard into music notation

Each of these capabilities can make the composer's work easier, but it is the composer who must make the final decision about what sounds best and is most musically appropriate.

Earth's Magnetic Field

by Charles Dodge

The earth is a giant magnet. Like other magnets, it has north and south poles and a magnetic field surrounding it. This magnetic field is constantly being altered by a force known as the solar wind (caused by changes in the sun's atmosphere). Scientists are able to record these magnetic field changes on a graph that looks similar to musical notation:

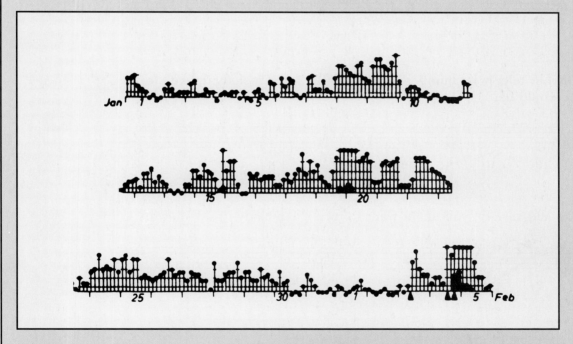

Charles Dodge (1942–) is a twentieth century American composer who specializes in computer music. Dodge converted information about the earth's magnetic field gathered during the year 1961 into a series of notes. Other musical decisions, including tempo, dynamics, and register, were also made with the help of the computer. The resulting music is titled "Earth's Magnetic Field." Without the aid of a computer, the conversion of this immense amount of information into music would not have been possible.

As you listen to the music, follow the graph above. Can you see a relationship between what you see and what you hear?

Convert Your Telephone Number Into Music

Using a similar method to the one used for "Earth's Magnetic Field," you can compose a piece of music using your telephone number and the computer. Each of the digits in your telephone number can be converted into a pitch. If you were to make this conversion without a computer, you might do it this way:

Assign one of the following pitches to each digit of your telephone number:

If your telephone number is 314-555-1212, the melody derived from it would be:

To add variety, you might want to turn the melody upside down:

Play it backwards:

Or play it upside down and backwards:

Composing With Tele-Music

To make this composition task easier, type the program called Tele-Music into your computer. Save the program on a disk, and use it to create a composition based on your telephone number. The computer will help you by

- converting the number into pitches (a melody)
- turning the melody upside down
- reversing the melody
- randomly adding rhythm to the melody
- changing the tempo of the melody to suit you
- playing the composition for you

Javanaise

by Claude Bolling

Listen to the music. Add a percussion part as indicated on the call chart below.

The music	Your percussion part
Introduction Piano opens with sounds in the middle register, separating quickly into opposite ends of the keyboard.	(whole rest symbol)
Section A The piano introduces a jaunty Theme A in $\frac{5}{4}$ meter, creating an uneven galloping motion.	sock cymbals $\frac{5}{4}$ bass drum (percussion notation)
Interlude The flute enters, playing sustained sounds moving stepwise, beginning low and reaching high.	(rub brush on cymbal using a circular motion to produce sustained sounds) (spiral symbol)
Section A (cont.) Theme A is now played by the flute with piano accompaniment.	s.c. $\frac{5}{4}$ b.d. (percussion notation)
Section B Percussion stops. Piano introduces Theme B. Flute and piano echo each other often. Theme A returns briefly as an interlude. Section B closes with rising piano octaves answered by a rapidly descending flute scale. piano flute	(whole rest symbol) s.c. $\frac{5}{4}$ b.d. (percussion notation) (whole rest symbol)

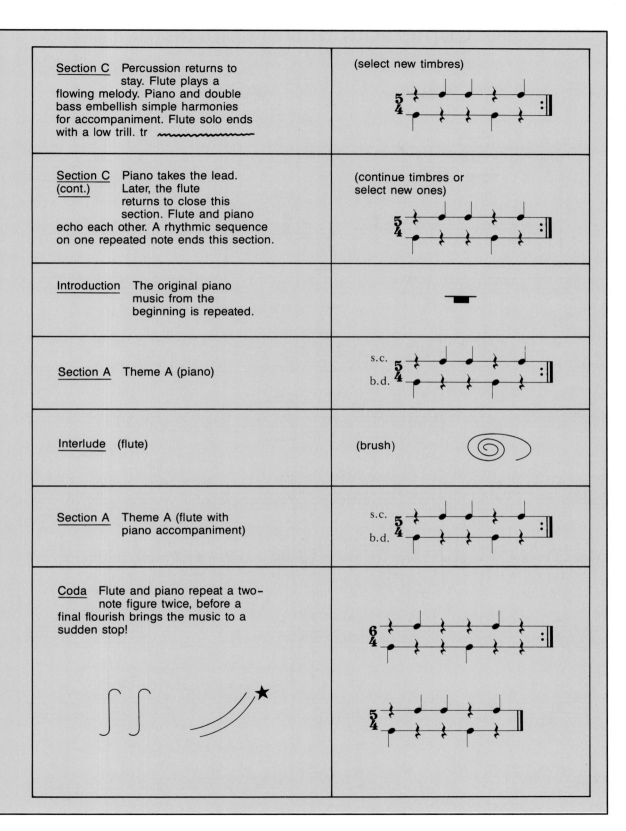

<u>Section C</u> Percussion returns to stay. Flute plays a flowing melody. Piano and double bass embellish simple harmonies for accompaniment. Flute solo ends with a low trill. tr 〰〰〰〰	(select new timbres)
<u>Section C</u> (cont.) Piano takes the lead. Later, the flute returns to close this section. Flute and piano echo each other. A rhythmic sequence on one repeated note ends this section.	(continue timbres or select new ones)
<u>Introduction</u> The original piano music from the beginning is repeated.	
<u>Section A</u> Theme A (piano)	s.c. b.d.
<u>Interlude</u> (flute)	(brush)
<u>Section A</u> Theme A (flute with piano accompaniment)	s.c. b.d.
<u>Coda</u> Flute and piano repeat a two-note figure twice, before a final flourish brings the music to a sudden stop!	

Come Join in the Chorus

Music by Wolfgang Amadeus Mozart

Unit 4

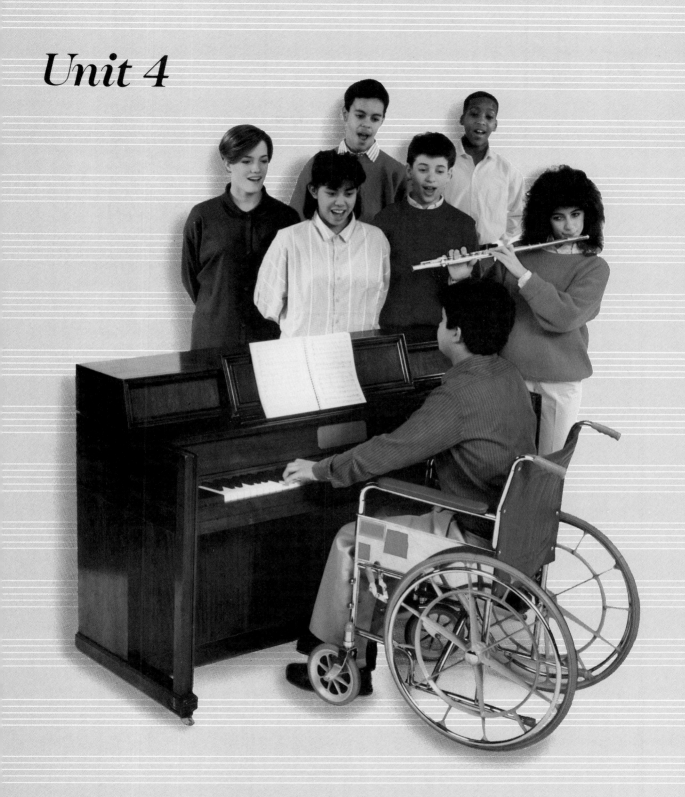

The Choral Sound

The Vocal Experience

In this unit you will have the opportunity to

- find the best part for your vocal range
- sing your part with a choral ensemble
- develop correct habits for supporting a good vocal sound
- train your ear to sing in tune with others
- develop good diction for singing
- sing within large and small ensembles
- sing in a variety of vocal styles

Begin by performing this song.
Which part will best fit your vocal range?

The Gift of Song

Words and Music by Patti Ingalls
Arranged by Buryl Red

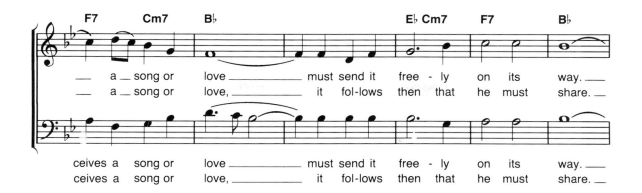

_a _ song or love _____ must send it free - ly on its way. __
_a _ song or love, _____ it fol-lows then that he must share. __

ceives a song or love _____ must send it free - ly on its way. __
ceives a song or love, _____ it fol-lows then that he must share. __

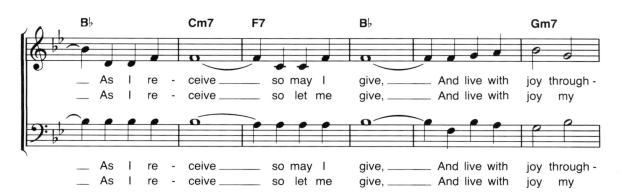

_ As I re - ceive _____ so may I give, _____ And live with joy through-
_ As I re - ceive _____ so let me give, _____ And live with joy my

_ As I re - ceive _____ so may I give, _____ And live with joy through-
_ As I re - ceive _____ so let me give, _____ And live with joy my

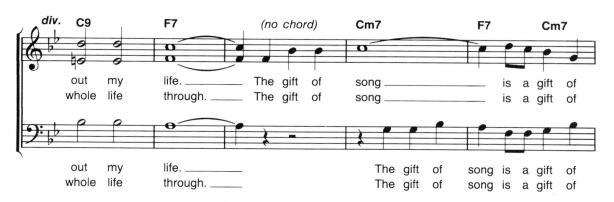

out my life. _____ The gift of song _____ is a gift of
whole life through. _____ The gift of song _____ is a gift of

out my life. _____ The gift of song is a gift of
whole life through. _____ The gift of song is a gift of

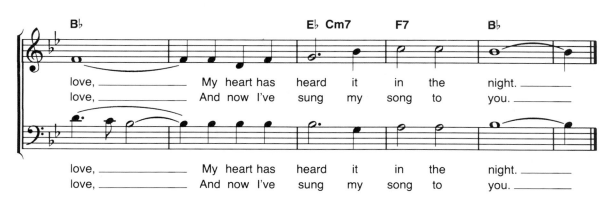

love, _____ My heart has heard it in the night. __
love, _____ And now I've sung my song to you. __

love, _____ My heart has heard it in the night. __
love, _____ And now I've sung my song to you. __

165

Who?

Scandinavian Folk Song

Melody: solo or small group

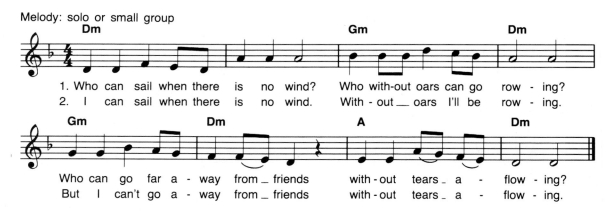

1. Who can sail when there is no wind? Who with-out oars can go row - ing?
2. I can sail when there is no wind. With - out __ oars I'll be row - ing.

Who can go far a - way from __ friends with - out tears __ a - flow - ing?
But I can't go a - way from __ friends with - out tears __ a - flow - ing.

Use these pitches to create harmony.   Tr. I
Tr. II
C.V.–Bar.

Add these parts to the melody.

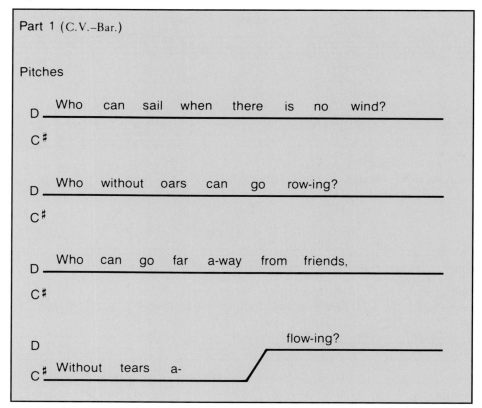

Part 1 (C.V.–Bar.)

Pitches

D — Who can sail when there is no wind?
C♯

D — Who without oars can go row-ing?
C♯

D — Who can go far a-way from friends,
C♯

D   flow-ing?
C♯ — Without tears a-

Part 2 (Tr. II)

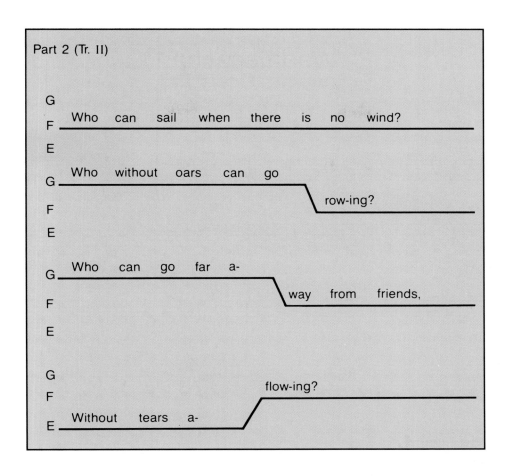

Part 3 (Tr. I)

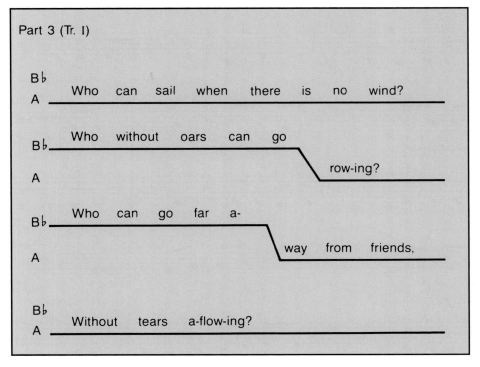

Wadaleeacha

Traditional

Tr. I Bar. (8ve lower)

Tr. II C.V.

Wa-da-lee-a-cha, wa-da-lee-a-cha, Doo-dle-dee-doo, _ doo-dle-dee-doo. _ Wa-da-lee-a-cha, wa-da-lee-a-cha, Doo-dle-dee-doo, _ doo-dle-dee-doo. _ Sim-plest thing, there is-n't much to _ it, All you got-ta do is doo-dle-dee-doo _ it. I like the rest of it, but what I like best _ is Doo-dle-dee, doo-dle-dee-doo. Yeah!

Aura Lee

American Folk Song
Arranged by Buryl Red

Learn to sing this two-part arrangement of a simple folk song.

Bye, Bye, Blues

Words and Music by Fred Hamm, Dave Bennett, Bert Lown, and Chauncey Gray

Clap or use the vocal sound "ch" to perform this "soft-shoe" rhythm:

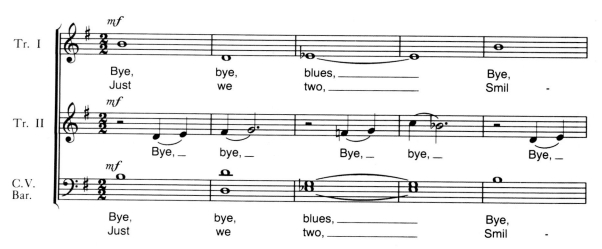

Tr. I — *mf*
Bye, bye, blues,_____ Bye,
Just we two,_____ Smil -

Tr. II — *mf*
Bye,__ bye,__ Bye,__ bye,__ Bye,__

C.V. Bar. — *mf*
Bye, bye, blues,_____ Bye,
Just we two,_____ Smil -

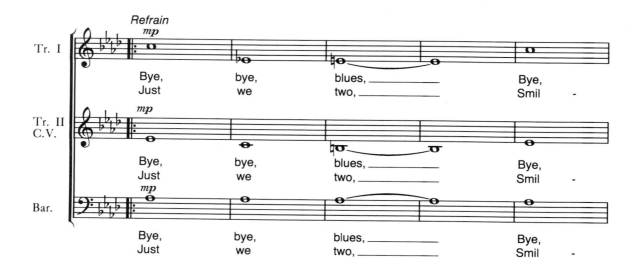

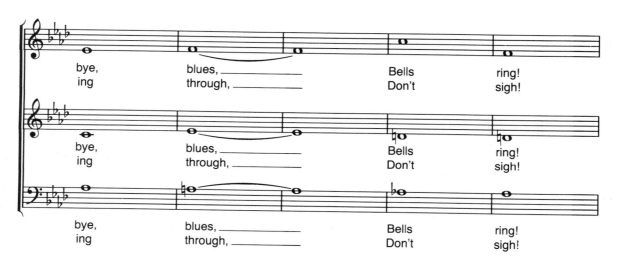

172

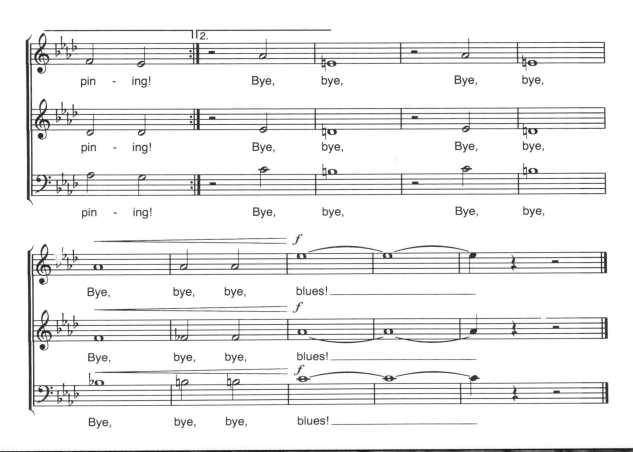

By the Light of the Silvery Moon

Words by Edward Madden

Music by Gus Edwards
Arranged by Buryl Red

This song and the next, "There's a Long, Long Trail," are typical of songs often performed by barbershop quartets in the early 1900s. Form your own small ensembles and perform these compositions for each other.

Two characteristics of barbershop style are chromatic harmonies and jazzy rhythmic interpretation. As you sing, turn this rhythm into

___ to my hon - ey I'll croon love's tune. Hon - ey

moon, to my hon - ey I'll croon, I'll croon love's tune. ___

moon, ___ keep a - shin - ing in June; ___

Hon - ey moon, hon - ey moon, keep a - shin - ing in June, the moon in

___ Your sil - very beams will bring love dreams, we'll be cud - dling

June; Your sil - very beams will bring love dreams, we'll be cud - dling

soon

soon, we'll cud - dle soon, by the sil - ver - y

soon, cud - dle soon, sil - very

Ritard
moon.

moon, and croon love's tune. ___

moon, and croon love's tune. ___

There's a Long, Long Trail

Words by Stoddard King

Music by Zo Elliot
Arranged by Buryl Red

Breathe only at the rests to maintain a flowing, *legato* sound.

176

* Cue size notes in the treble clef may be played on any instrument, in any range, or they may be hummed by a solo voice or whistled.

177

Factory Fantasia

by Jay W. Gilbert

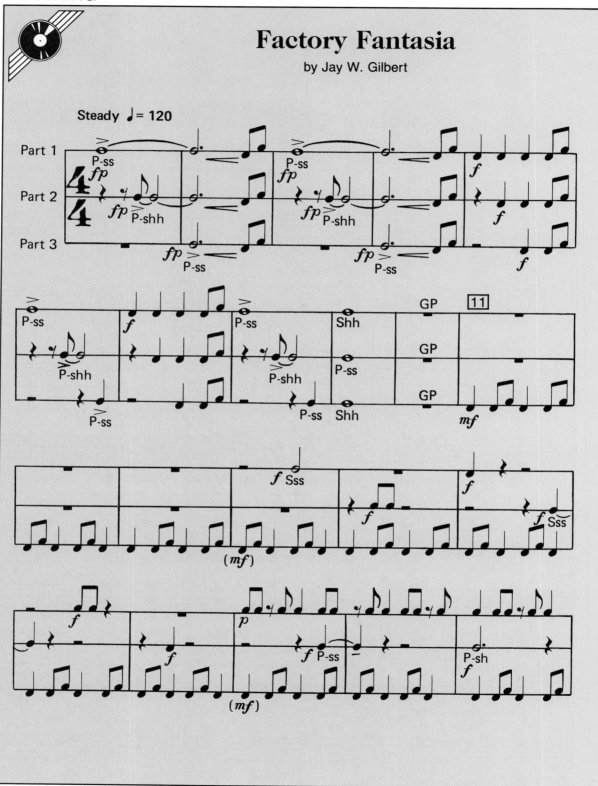

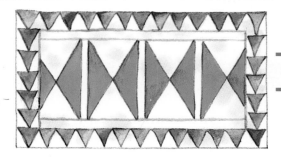

Missa

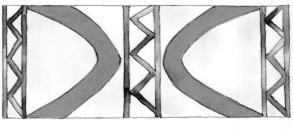

Words and Music by Neil Diamond

Standin' on the Walls of Zion

Words Traditional

Music by Maurice Gardner

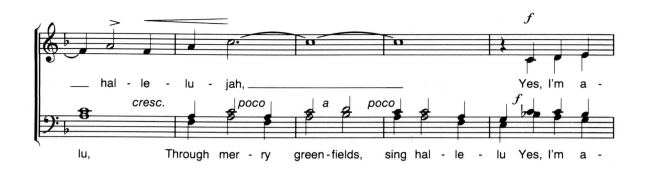

_hal - le - lu - jah, _____ Yes, I'm a -

cresc. _poco_ _a_ _poco_

lu,   Through mer - ry green - fields,   sing hal - le - lu   Yes, I'm a -

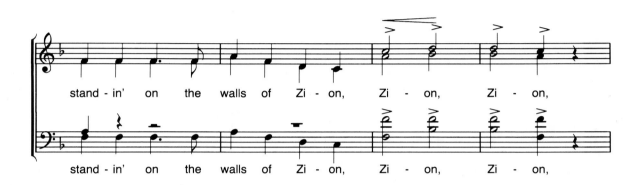

stand - in' on the walls of Zi - on,   Zi - on,   Zi - on,

stand - in' on the walls of Zi - on,   Zi - on,   Zi - on,

Saw my ship a - sail - in' home, _ Zi - on,   Zi - on.

Saw my ship a - sail - in' home, _ Zi - on,   Zi - on.

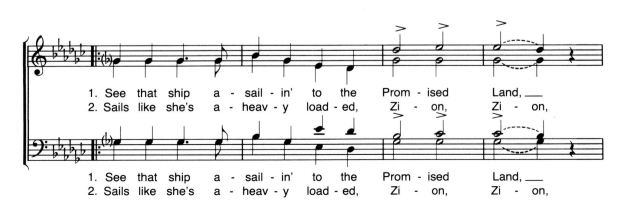

1. See that ship a - sail - in' to the Prom - ised   Land, _
2. Sails like she's a - heav - y load - ed,   Zi - on,   Zi - on,

1. See that ship a - sail - in' to the Prom - ised   Land, _
2. Sails like she's a - heav - y load - ed,   Zi - on,   Zi - on,

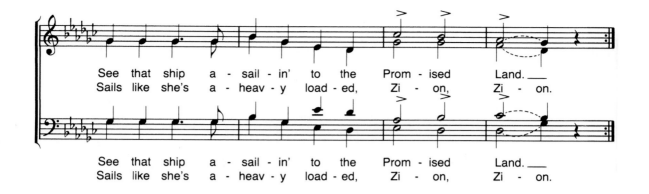

See that ship a - sail - in' to the Prom - ised Land. ___
Sails like she's a - heav - y load - ed, Zi - on, Zi - on.

See that ship a - sail - in' to the Prom - ised Land. ___
Sails like she's a - heav - y load - ed, Zi - on, Zi - on.

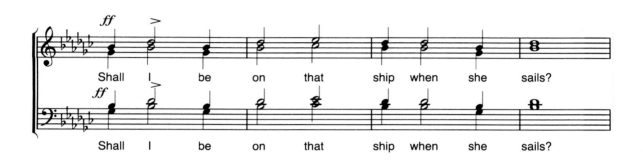

Shall I be on that ship when she sails?

Shall I be on that ship when she sails?

Shall I be on that ship when she sails? Yes I'm a -

Shall I be on that ship when she sails? Yes, I'm a -

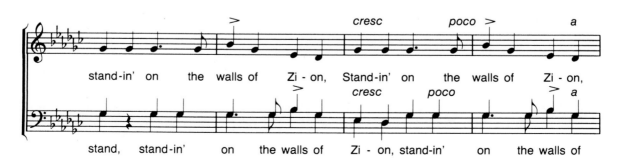

stand-in' on the walls of Zi - on, Stand-in' on the walls of Zi - on,

stand, stand-in' on the walls of Zi - on, stand-in' on the walls of

186

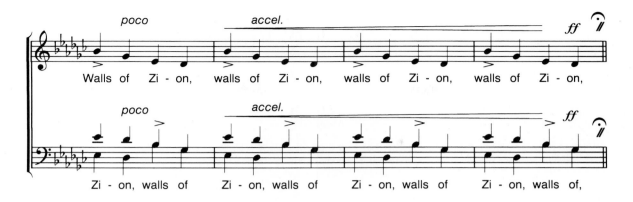

Walls of Zi - on, walls of Zi - on, walls of Zi - on, walls of Zi - on,

Zi - on, walls of Zi - on, walls of Zi - on, walls of Zi - on, walls of,

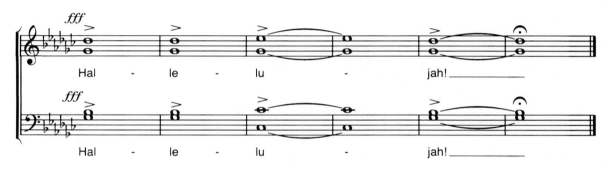

Hal - le - lu - jah!

Hal - le - lu - jah!

Hyda

Israeli Round

1. Hy - da, hy - da, hy - da-da hy - da, Hy - da, Hy - da, hy - da;

2. Hy - da, hy - da-da hy - da, hy - da, hy - da, hy - da.

3. Hy - da, hy - da-da hy - da, Hy - da, hy - da, hy - da.

Roll On, Columbia

Words and Music by Woody Guthrie

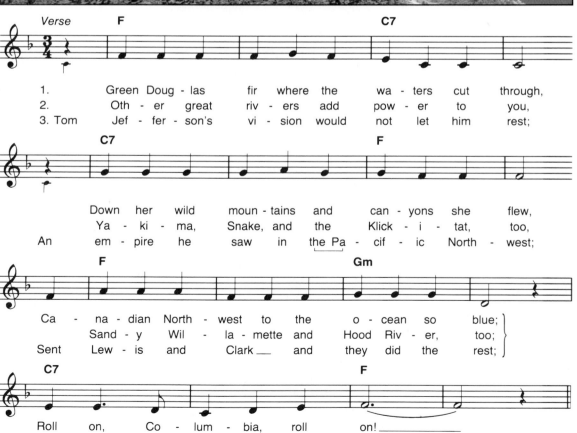

Verse

F   **C7**

1.   Green Doug - las   fir where the   wa - ters   cut   through,
2.   Oth - er great   riv - ers add   pow - er   to   you,
3. Tom Jef - fer - son's   vi - sion would   not let him   rest;

C7   **F**

Down her   wild   moun - tains and   can - yons she   flew,
Ya - ki - ma,   Snake, and the   Klick - i - tat,   too,
An em - pire he   saw in the Pa - cif - ic North - west;

F   **Gm**

Ca - na - dian North - west to the   o - cean so   blue;
Sand - y Wil - la - mette and   Hood Riv - er,   too;
Sent Lew - is and   Clark   and they did the   rest;

C7   **F**

Roll on, Co - lum - bia, roll   on! ___

4. At Bonneville now there are ships in the locks;
   The waters have risen and cleared all the rocks.
   Shiploads of plenty will steam past the docks;
   Roll on, Columbia, roll on!
   Refrain

5. And on up the river is Grand Coulee Dam,
   The mightiest thing ever built by a man,
   To run the great fact'ries and water the land;
   Roll on, Columbia, roll on!
   Refrain

Freedom

Words by Peter Udell   **Music by Gary Geld**

Learn to sing this song. How will you perform it? What kind of vocal style would be appropriate?

FREEDOM, from Shenandoah,
Lyric by Peter Udell. Music by Gary Geld
© 1974, 1975 GARY GELD and PETER UDELL
All Rights Controlled by EDWIN H. MORRIS & COMPANY, a division of MPL Communications, Inc.
International Copyright Secured All Rights Reserved Used by Permission

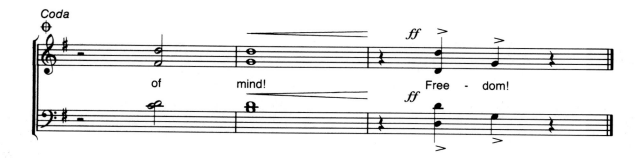

One of Those Songs

Words by Will Holt

Music by Gerald Calvi

The first four phrases of this melody are the same.
How does the composer keep these same repeated ideas from becoming dull and monotonous?

Follow

Words and Music by Jack Noble White
Arranged by Buryl Red

be when I fol-low __ you. Don't just tag a-long, fol-low some-thing strong,

be when I _____ fol-low you. Don't tag a - long,

fol-low, __ fol-low, __

fol - low, _____ Then you'll al-ways find you're not left be-hind,

fol - low, fol - low, Then you'll

fol-low, __ fol-low, __

fol - low, _____ Oh, fol - low your heart and then just

fol - low, fol - low your heart, _____

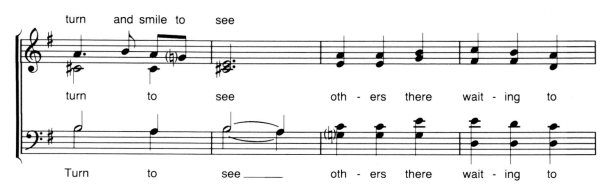

turn and smile to see

turn to see oth - ers there wait - ing to

Turn to see _____ oth - ers there wait - ing to

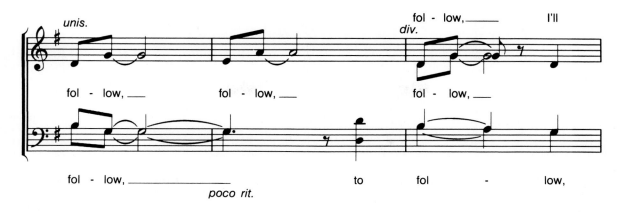

fol - low,_____ I'll

fol - low,___ fol - low,___ fol - low,___

fol - low,_____ to fol - low,

poco rit.

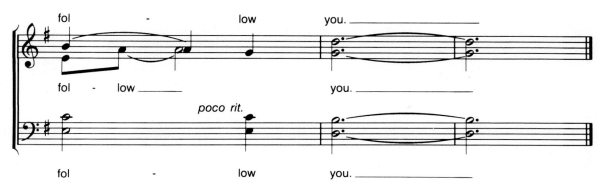

fol - low you._____

fol - low_____ you.

poco rit.

fol - low you._____

Canción de La Luna

Traditional Mexican Folk Song

Verse

unison A E7 A D A

Tr. I
Tr. II

1. A las dos de la ma - ña - na Que le vengo a des-per - tas,
2. Con vio - li - nes y gui - tar-ras Yo te vine a sal - u - dar.

Refrain
div. unis. A E7 A D A

C.V.
Bar.

Des-pier - ta, mi bien, des - pier - ta, Des-pier - ta ya aman-e - ció;
Ya los pa - ja-ros can - tar - ón Y la lu - na se me - tió.

El Cumbanchero

Words and Music by Rafael Hernandez

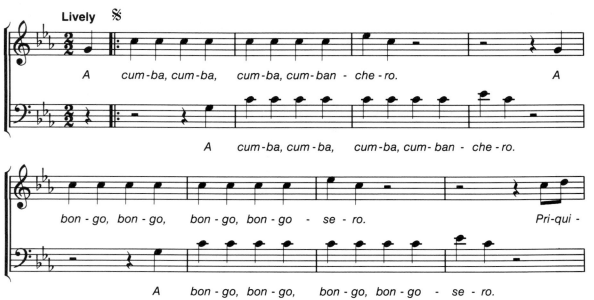

Lively 𝄋

A cum-ba, cum-ba, cum-ba, cum-ban-che-ro. A

A cum-ba, cum-ba, cum-ba, cum-ban-che-ro.

bon-go, bon-go, bon-go, bon-go-se-ro. Pri-qui-

A bon-go, bon-go, bon-go, bon-go-se-ro.

ti que va so - an-do el cum-ban - che-ro bon-go - se-ro que se va,

Cum - cum - cum - cum - cum - cum - cum - cum - cum.

To Coda

1.
bon-go-se-ro que se va. _____ A va. _____

Cum-ba, cum-ba, cum-ba, cum. Cum-ba, cum-ba, cum.

Tr. I

el tam - bor _ bi-ri-qui - ti, _____

Tr. I
Tr. II
(Div.)

sue-ña a - si el tam - bor, _ ti, _____

C.V.
Bar.

Y sue - ña a - si el tam - bor, _ ti, _____ bum-bum -

bum-bum - ba. re - pi -

bum-bum - ba. vuel - ve a re - pi -

ba. Y vuel - ve a re - pi -

Matilda

Traditional
Adapted by Massie Patterson and Sammy Heyward

Laredo

Traditional Mexican Folk Song

Tr. I / Tr. II

I leave now to go to La-re-do, my love, I come here to say fare-well. _
While I'm there I will sore-ly __ miss you, my love, how much I can nev-er tell. _
Ya me voy pa-ra el La-re-do, mi bien, Te ven-go a de-cir a-diós. _
De a-llá te man-do de-cir, __ mi bien, co-mo se man-cuer-nan dos. _

And this gold-en key, now take it, my love, and o-pen my se-cret heart: _
How much I shall al-ways want you, my love, and how great my pain to part. __
To-ma e-sa lla-vi-ta de o-ro, mi bien, ab-re mi pe-cho y ver-ás: ___
Lo mu-cho que yo te quie-ro, mi bien, y el mal pa-go que me das. __

And take now the chest of treas-ures, my love, and all that it may con-tain. _
It holds all my great de-vo-tion, my love, my pas-sion and some-times pain. _
To-ma e-sa ca-ji-ta de o-ro, mi bien, mi-ra lo que lle-va den-tro. __
Lle-va a-mo-res, lle-va ce-los, mi bien, y un po-co de sen-ti-mien-to. __

I leave now to go to La-re-do, my love, I come here to say fare-well. __
Ya me voy pa-ra el La-re-do, mi bien, Te ven-go a de-cir a-diós. __

While I'm there, I will sore-ly miss you, my love, how much I can nev-er tell._____

De a - llá te man-do de - cir,___ mi bien, co - mo se man-cuer-nan dos._____

div. unis.

LISTENING

El Salón México

(excerpt)

by Aaron Copland

Clap these patterns.

Which of these patterns is most like "Laredo"?
Which of these patterns is most like the "Laredo"
melody heard in *El Salón México?*

Sigh No More, Ladies, Sigh No More!

Words by William Shakespeare

Music by Emma Lou Diemer

one ___ on shore, and one ___ on shore; To one ___ thing con - stant

one ___ on shore, and one ___ on shore; To one ___ thing con - stant

shore, and one ___ on shore, and one ___ on shore;

nev - er. But let ___ them go, And be ___ you blithe ___ and

nev - er.

Then sigh ___ not so, And be ___ you blithe ___ and

bon - ny, Con - vert - ing your sounds of woe _____ In - to

bon - ny, Con - vert - ing your sounds of woe _____ In - to

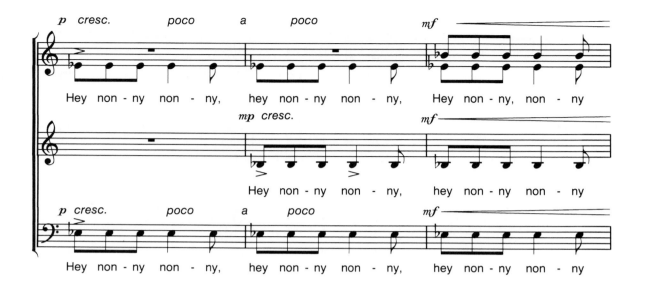

Hey non - ny non - ny, hey non - ny non - ny, Hey non - ny, non - ny

Hey non - ny non - ny, hey non - ny non - ny

Hey non - ny non - ny, hey non - ny non - ny, hey non - ny non - ny

hey! ___ Sing no more dit - ties, sing _ no more, sing _ no more, _ no

hey! ___ Sing no more dit - ties, sing _ no more,

hey! ___ Sing no more dit - ties, sing _ no more, sing _ no more, _ no

more _____ of dumps _ so dull and heav - y!

more _____ of dumps _ so dull and heav - y! Fraud _ of

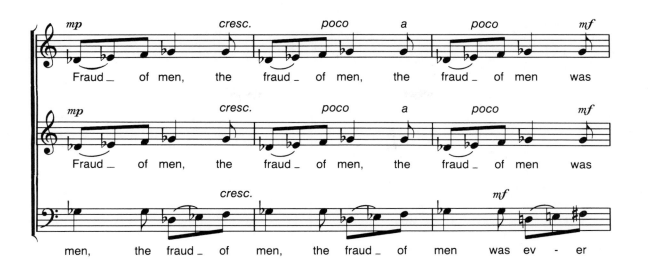

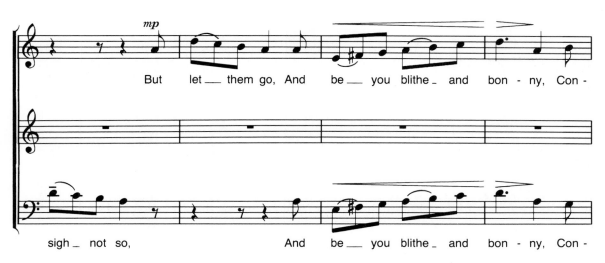

vert-ing your sounds of woe ———— In - to

mp
Hey non - ny

vert-ing your sounds of woe ———— In - to Hey non - ny non - ny,

cresc. *poco* *a* *poco*
Hey non-ny non - ny, hey non-ny non - ny, hey non-ny,

Hey non - ny non - ny, hey non-ny non - ny, hey non-ny non - ny,

cresc. *poco* *a* *poco*
non - ny, hey non-ny non - ny, hey non-ny, non - ny, hey non-ny,

cresc. *poco* *a* *poco*
Hey non-ny non - ny, hey non-ny non - ny, hey non-ny non - ny,

f
hey non - ny non - ny hey! ————

f
hey non - ny non - ny hey! ————

f
hey non - ny non - ny hey! ————

Sheep Safely Graze

Words by Eloise Williams

Music by Johann Sebastian Bach

The Sleigh

Music by Richard Kountz
Arranged by W. Riegger

209

(cres.) *poco a poco*

o'er the snow, With a hey, hah, hah, Ho, hah, Gai - ly sing - ing,

(cres.) *poco a poco*

hey, hah, hah, Ho, hah, hah, hah, ho, hah, ho, hah,

(cres.) *poco a poco*

o'er the snow, With sleigh-bells ring - ing, ho, hah, ho, hah,

(cres.) *poco a poco*

o'er the snow, With a hey, hah, hey, hah, ho, hah, ho, hah,

f

Mer - ri - ly we go, Ho, hal - lo! Mer - ri - ly on we go. Ho, hal - lo!

f

Mer - ri - ly we go, Ho, hal - lo! Mer - ri - ly on we go. Ho, hal - lo!

f

Mer - ri - ly we go, Ho, hal - lo! Mer - ri - ly on we go. Ho, hal - lo!

f

Mer - ri - ly we go, Ho, hal - lo! Mer - ri - ly on we go. Ho, hal - lo!

A Christmas Happening

Music by Buryl Red

By the Waters Babylon

Traditional Round

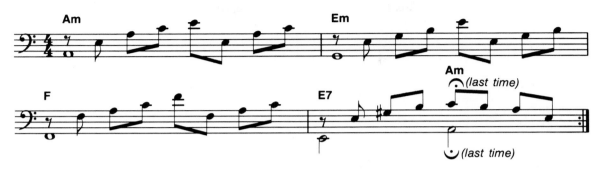

Divide into groups. Sing all the parts of this song in canon, or sing only the part suitable for your voice range as an ostinato.

Can the ground bass shown above be used to accompany this canon? How do you know?

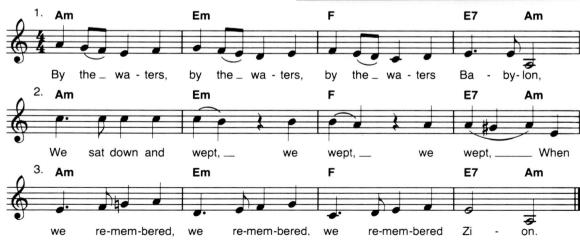

1. By the — wa - ters, by the — wa - ters, by the — wa - ters Ba - by - lon,

2. We sat down and wept, — we wept, — we wept, _____ When

3. we re-mem-bered, we re-mem-bered, we re-mem-bered Zi - on.

215

Grab Another Hand

Traditional

2. Shake another hand, shake a hand next to ya, etc.

3. Clap another hand, clap a hand next to ya, etc.

4. Raise another hand, raise a hand next to ya, etc.

5. Hug another friend, hug a friend next to ya, etc.

Now Comes the Hour

Music by Ludwig van Beethoven

Ludwig van Beethoven was born in the city of Bonn, Germany, in 1770. From 1792 Beethoven's artistic fame never stopped growing, despite the fact that during this time he became totally deaf. When he died in 1827, Beethoven was esteemed as the world's greatest composer. His genius brought the Classical tradition to its height and opened the door to the Romantic era. Among his many works are nine symphonies, 18 string quartets, 32 piano sonatas, and numerous other pieces for piano and for various vocal and instrumental ensembles.

1. Now comes the hour for peace-ful rest, Oh, how blest peace-ful __ rest!

2. Ah, (or hum) _____ Ah _____ peace - ful rest!

3. Now comes the hour for peace - ful __ rest, Oh, how blest __ peace-ful rest!

Let the Sun Shine In

Words by James Rado and Jerome Ragni

Music by Galt MacDermot

Glossary

Accent   a sound performed more heavily than other sounds, *62*

Aeolian   a mode of seven pitches whose scale (by whole and half steps) is W W H W H W W, *138*

Andante   at a medium (walking) speed, *207*

Arranging   taking existing music and creating special parts for instruments and voices, *23*

Articulation   how sounds begin and end when they are performed, *19*

Beat   the steady pulse that underlies most music, *149*

Blue note   usually the third or seventh degrees of a scale, bent or otherwise altered so the pitch is between major and minor, *153*

Brass family   wind instruments made of brass or other metal including the trumpet, French horn, trombone, and tuba, *58*

Canon   a form of imitation in which each part plays or sings the same melody at different times; a round, *122*

Central pitch   scale step 1, or the pitch to which all other pitches appear to return, *67*

Charleston   an American dance originally popularized in the 1920's, *65*

Chord   three or more pitches occurring at the same time, *151*

Choreographer   someone who creates dance movements, usually to musical accompaniment, *22*

Chromaticism   the use of pitches that would not usually be used in a given key or scale, *58*

Claves   a Latin-American percussion instrument consisting of two sticks that are struck together, *132*

Coda   a closing section of a musical composition, *9*

Composing   the act of creating and notating new and original music, *10*

Contrary motion   the movement of two voice parts in opposite directions, *71*

Dorian   a mode of seven pitches whose scale, in terms of whole and half steps, is W H W W W H W, *81*

Dynamics   the degrees of loudness and softness in music, *59*

Ground bass   a repeating bass pattern, *122*

Harmony   a series of chords in a given piece of music, *154*

Homophony   music in which a melody is accompanied by other voices, generally moving in the same rhythm, *68*

Improvising   the act of performing music "on the spot" without the aid of notation, *119*

Ionian   a mode of seven pitches whose scale, in terms of whole and half steps, is W W H W W W H, *139*

Jazz   a distinctive style of American music developed from ragtime and blues, *151*

Legato   performed in a smooth, connected manner, *176*

Major scale   a scale of seven pitches ordered, in terms of whole and half steps, as W W H W W W H, *139*

Melody   a series of pitches arranged rhythmically to create a musical line, *66*

Meter signature   a sign consisting of two numbers found at the beginning of a piece of music or section; indicates the number and type of beat found in each measure, *146*

Minuet   a popular dance of the seventeenth and eighteenth centuries, based on a meter signature of 3/4 and performed at a moderate tempo, *64*

Miracle play   a medieval religious drama based on the lives of the saints, *74*

Mixolydian   a mode of seven pitches whose scale, in terms of whole and half steps, is W W H W W H W, *141*

Mode   a specific arrangement of pitches to form a scale; usually refers to medieval church modes, *138*

Monophony   a single musical line, *68*

Motion   changing pitch levels in a melody, *66*

Notation   a way of writing down music, *126*

Opera   an art work encompassing music, drama, and visual design, *58*

Ornament   a standard type of melodic embellishment (such as a trill, etc.), *154*

Ostinato   a musical pattern or figure repeated over and over, *123*

Parallel motion   the same or a similar musical line performed simultaneously at a different pitch, *71*

Pavane   a slow court dance of the sixteenth century, usually performed in a meter signature based on four beats, *64*

Mixolydian a mode of seven pitches whose scale, in terms of whole and half steps, is W W H W W H W

Mode a specific arrangement of pitches to form a scale; usually refers to medieval church modes

Moderato at a moderate speed

Modulation the change in harmony from one key to another in a musical composition

Monophony a single musical line

Motive (motif) the smallest rhythmic, melodic, or harmonic unit of a musical theme that can be identified

Movement a complete and independent section of a musical composition

Note a sign that shows the pitch and the length of a tone

Ornament a standard type of melodic embellishment (such as a trill, etc.)

Ostinato a musical pattern or figure repeated over and over

Parallel motion the same or a similar musical line performed simultaneously at a different pitch

Pentatonic a scale of five pitches with no half steps between any two pitches; occurs when only the black keys on the piano are used

Phrase a grouping of notes that forms a musical sentence

Pitch the highness or lowness of a musical pitch

Polyphony music in which two or more independent melody lines occur at the same time

Presto at a very fast speed

Ritardando a gradual slowing of the tempo

Scale an arrangement of tones by pitch according to the order of whole steps and half steps

Staccato performed in a short, separated manner

Syncopation a shift of accent from the strong beat to the weak beat in music

Tablature a system of instrumental notation indicating the string, fret, key, or finger to be used, instead of the pitch to be played

Tempo the speed at which the beat moves in music

Texture the consistency of the "fabric" of music; such as thickness, thinness, etc.

Theme a melody or phrase used as basic material for a musical composition

Timbre the quality or color of a sound

Tonal center usually the central pitch in a given key

Tone color see **timbre**

Tonic the first pitch of a scale; or chord of a given key

Transcribe (transcription *n.*) to transfer from one performing medium to another; for example, a piano transcription made of an orchestral composition

Variation a musical idea that is repeated with some change

Vibrato a quality of sound produced by small, rapid variations in pitch; executed in string instruments by a rapid movement of the left hand

Acknowledgments

Grateful acknowledgment is made to the following copyright owners and agents for their permission to reprint the following copyrighted material. Every effort has been made to locate all copyright owners; any errors or omissions in copyright notice are inadvertent and will be corrected as they are discovered.

"Amen," arranged by Marion Downs, from *Junior High Sings*. Adapted and reprinted by permission of World Around Songs.

"Aura Lee," American folk song, arranged by Buryl Red. Copyright © 1980 Generic Music. Reprinted by permission.

"Bells and Pachelbels," by Buryl Red. Copyright © 1986 by Generic Music. Reprinted by permission.

"The Boys," words and music by Roger Miller. Copyright © 1985 by Tree Publishing Co., Inc. and Roger Miller Music, 8 Music Square West, Nashville, TN 37203. International Copyright Secured. ALL RIGHTS RESERVED. Reprinted by Permission of Hal Leonard Publishing Corportion.

"By the Light of the Silvery Moon," words by Ed Madden, music by Gus Edwards. Copyright © 1909 (Renewed) WARNER BROS. INC. All Rights Reserved. Reprinted by Permission.

"Bye, Bye Blues," by Fred Hamm, Dave Bennett, Bert Lown and Chauncey Gray. © Copyright 1925, 1930, 1962 by Bourne Co., Music Publishers. Copyright renewed. Reprinted by permission.

"Can the Circle Be Unbroken," adapted and arranged by Dan Fox. This Arrangement Copyright © 1978 Cherry Lane Music Co., Inc. International Copyright Secured. All Rights Reserved. Reprinted by Permission.

"Carry It On," words and music by Gil Turner. TRO—Copyright 1954 and 1965 Melody Trails, Inc., New York, NY. Reprinted by Permission of the Richmond Organization.

"A Christmas Happening," by Buryl Red, copyright © 1970 by Generic Music. Reprinted by permission.

"Come Join in the Chorus," music from "The Magic Flute" by Mozart, words from *The Three-Way Chorister* by Maurice Gardner, copyright © 1957 by Staff Music Publishing Company. Reprinted by permission.

"The Cruel War," by Paul Stookey and Peter Yarrow. © 1962 PEPAMAR MUSIC CORP. All Rights Reserved. Reprinted by Permission of Warner Bros. Music Corp.

"El Cumbanchero," Spanish words and music by Rafael Hernandez. Copyright © 1943 (Renewed) by Peer International Corporation. Reprinted by permission of Columbia Pictures Publications.

Art Credits

Photo Credits

Alphabetical Index of Music

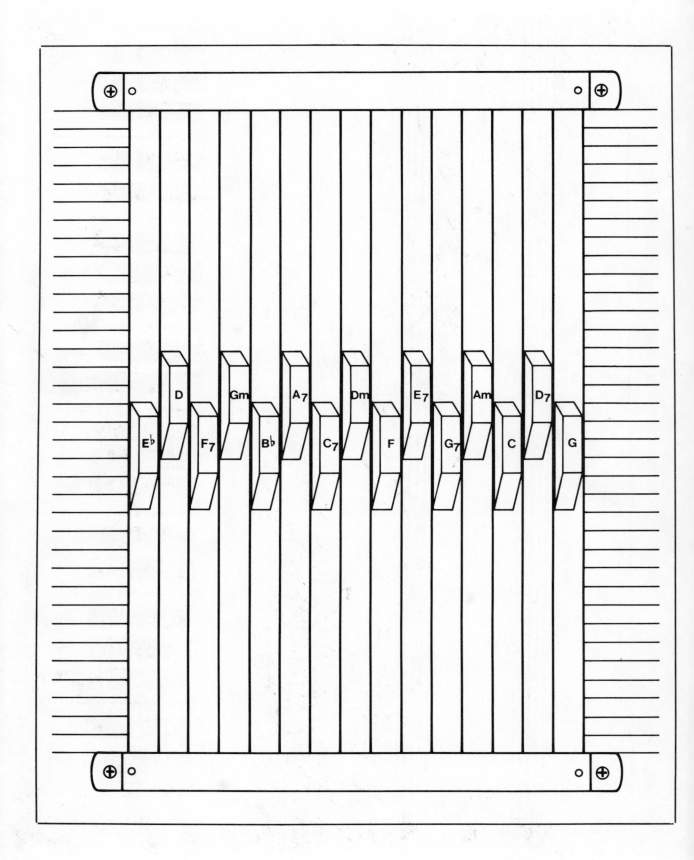